“It’s ok [illegible] u to a hos[illegible] on.”

The man made a noise that sounded an awful lot like “no,” but that couldn’t be right. Maybe the poor bastard was out of his head. Joe leaned in when the guy lifted his head. “No cops,” he slurred, tightening his grip on Joe’s arm, his voice so low and gravelly Joe wouldn’t have heard him if he hadn’t been so close. “No hospital.”

“What?” Joe shook his head and did his best to remain calm. “Listen, buddy, someone knocked you over the head. You need medical attention.”

“Please, no cops. Help me.”

“I’m trying to help, but the best I can do is get you to a hospital. I’m not a doctor.”

“They’ll… kill me. Cops… dead…. No hospital. Please.” With that, the guy collapsed back onto the ground.

Well, those were certainly words he didn’t care to hear in the same sentence.

Charlie Cochet

Forgive and Forget

Published by

Published by
DREAMSPINNER PRESS

5032 Capital Circle SW, Suite 2, PMB# 279,
Tallahassee, FL 32305-7886 USA
www.dreamspinnerpress.com

This is a work of fiction. Names, characters, places, and incidents either are the product of author imagination or are used fictitiously, and any resemblance to actual persons, living or dead, business establishments, events, or locales is entirely coincidental.

Cover content is for illustrative purposes only and any person depicted on the cover is a model.

ISBN: 978-1-63477-016-3
Digital ISBN: 978-1-63477-017-0
Library of Congress Control Number: 2015917563
Published April 2016
v. 1.0

Printed in the United States of America

This paper meets the requirements of
ANSI/NISO Z39.48-1992 (Permanence of Paper).

CHARLIE COCHET is an author by day and artist by night. Always quick to succumb to the whispers of her wayward muse, no star is out of reach when following her passion. From adventurous agents and sexy shifters to society gentlemen and hardboiled detectives, there's bound to be plenty of mischief for her heroes to find themselves in—and plenty of romance, too!

Currently residing in Central Florida, Charlie is at the beck and call of a rascally Doxiepoo bent on world domination. When she isn't writing, she can usually be found reading, drawing, or watching movies. She runs on coffee, thrives on music, and loves to hear from readers.

Website: www.charliecochet.com
Blog: www.charliecochet.com/blog
E-mail: charlie@charliecochet.com
Facebook: www.facebook.com/charliecochet
Twitter: @charliecochet
Tumblr: www.charliecochet.tumblr.com
Pinterest: www.pinterest.com/charliecochet
Goodreads: www.goodreads.com/CharlieCochet
THIRDS HQ: www.thirdshq.com

Thank you to all my wonderful readers, to Dreamspinner Press, and the amazing people in my life who are always there to offer support, love, and guidance.

Chapter One

"**JOE!** You're killing me!"

The low growl melted into a moan of satisfaction, bringing a hearty laugh from Joe. "It's just apple pie, Mr. Richardson." He refilled the wily old man's coffee mug and received a bushy-browed scowl in return.

"The hell it is, son. If it was any old apple pie, you think I'd bother walking eight city blocks to get here? You're too damned modest, Joe. Everyone knows you make the best damn pies in the city, probably all of New York State!"

Joe didn't know about the entirety of New York, but seeing how happy his pies made Mr. Richardson was more than enough for him. Apple'n Pies wasn't big or fancy, by any means. It was a cozy little hole-in-the-wall six blocks from Times Square, free of all the fancy coffee machines, exotic flavors, or overpriced merchandise. It was all his, and it was home.

Wiping his hands on his apron, Joe took a moment to survey his little kingdom of baked goods and java. The wooden floorboards and medium-sized counter were scuffed, the old oak frames of the booths just as worn, but solid and polished, the red upholstery always clean and without tears. What little chrome there was came from the stools at the counter, which had been installed a couple of years ago after one of his regulars had gone straight through one of the old ones. He could hardly have customers falling through the furniture now, could he?

The silver of the stools matched the shelving units of the back counter, which housed the tableware, and in the far corner was Rusty—a cash register that looked like it belonged back in the Civil War days. Bea was always telling him to get rid of it, but Joe didn't have the heart. Besides, Rusty was still as sturdy and reliable as ever, even if the drawer did stick sometimes and Bea had taken a baseball bat to it on more than one occasion. Of course, the dinged-up baseball bat always came out of the scuffle worse off than Rusty.

The place was reminiscent of one of those old vintage cafés. It was old-school, but it was spotless, tidy, and most importantly, filled with happy customers treating themselves to his pies. In the corner, Dean Martin's "Powder Your Face with Sunshine" floated up from the old radio.

Some men wanted to be doctors, lawyers, movie stars, or millionaires. Joe was happy baking pies, and when his customers were happy, he was happy, and they were happy with a little help from him. What more could a guy ask for?

The little brass bell above the glass-paned door jingled, and Joe cheerfully went to meet his new customers. Outside, the world was moving at rocket speed, with no time to spare for those who hadn't the means or the heart to keep up. Apple'n Pies provided a quiet, safe haven for anyone who needed it, from Hollywood movie stars to youngsters down from the local Y. Everyone was welcome at Joe's.

Joe greeted a young couple with a cheery "Good morning" before showing the couple to an empty booth.

The handsome pair looked like they'd stepped out of a fashion magazine. Their gazes darted around the place with noticeable uncertainty. It was pretty obvious it wasn't their typical coffee stop. Joe never took offense. Instead, he smiled warmly and got busy making them feel at home.

"I'm Joe Applin. Welcome to my little corner of pie paradise. I'll be happy to get you anything you like. While you're under my roof, you're in good hands."

The young woman's face lit up as her companion helped her out of her long expensive coat. "Oh! Applin, as in *Apple'n*! That's you!" She giggled, and Joe felt his dopey grin get dopier. He never tired of people's fascination with his name and how it suited his profession. Of course, it had been his family name long before he'd ever learned what a pie was.

"I hope apple is your favorite," she chirped, clapping her hands joyously when he nodded. It was actually cherry, but who was he to burst her bubble? The pair slid into the booth and didn't bother with the menu. "Father says your coffee's almost as good as your pies. He comes in here all the time. Works just down the road at Jameson and Rotherford's. It's a law firm." The young man at her side simply smiled fondly while his sweetheart held the reins on the conversation. "His name's Allan Rotherford. My father, that is. Do you know him?"

"Of course, miss." Mr. Rotherford came in every afternoon to take a slice of pie back to the office with him. After the fifth time, half the firm was in during various parts of the day, sneaking confectionary goodies back to their desks. "He's particularly fond of the apple and cinnamon."

"I tell you, Joe—may I call you Joe?" she asked hopefully. He nodded and she squealed with delight. "Well, Joe. Father's been going on and on about your pies for weeks! I had to see for myself what all the fuss was about. He was driving me and my poor mother absolutely crazy. So," she said with a decisive nod, "two apple and cinnamon pies, and two coffees."

"Right away, miss. And when you're finished, I'd love to hear if you enjoyed it as much as your father." That seemed to make her even happier, and she nodded enthusiastically.

As he walked away, she chatted to her boyfriend at full speed, bringing a smile to Joe's face. The guy was obviously smitten, seeing as how he wasn't the least bit concerned about getting a word in edgewise. Removing the heavy glass dome over the apple and cinnamon pie dish, Joe cut out two generous slices and moved them onto two immaculate, white ceramic dishes. He dropped them off at the table along with their coffee, exchanged a few more pleasantries, then excused himself so the pair could enjoy their food. He barely made it to the counter when a loud crash echoed from the kitchen out back.

Here we go.

The door slammed open and Donnie scrambled out, nearly tripping over his own feet before he made a dive behind Joe. There were a few curious glances from some of the newer patrons, but the regulars were used to the daily disturbances brought about by the terrible trio Joe called family. Soon everyone's attention returned to their newspapers and coffee.

"Joe, she's trying to kill me!" Donnie's voice went higher in pitch with every word uttered, and he clutched Joe's forearms in what Joe assumed was meant to be some kind of death grip. In reality it was about as deadly as a kitten swatting at a ball of yarn.

Looking at the kid, it was hard to believe he was eighteen years old. Donnie stilled, most likely knowing Joe's broader, six-foot frame would eclipse him. When Joe felt Donnie remove his hands, he knew the eclipsing was complete, and none too soon either. The kitchen door swung open, and Bea stomped out in all her gray-haired glory. Joe couldn't blame the kid for hiding. He wanted to hide too.

"Where is he," Bea demanded, folding her arms over her heaving bosom. She peered at him with her sharp green eyes. Joe knew better than to risk his life by incurring the old woman's wrath, but he just couldn't find it in him to turn the kid over. Bea was in her sixties, stout, hair pulled back tight in a bun, and had the power to command more fear than a military general. Not to mention, her batting average was probably better than any major league player's.

"Bea, angel, what can I do for you?" Joe moved slowly in the opposite direction, and with every step she took, Donnie moved with him.

"Don't you *angel* me, Joe Applin. I know you're hiding him. If you're not looking to get a good butt whooping yourself, you'll hand him over."

Joe knew full well she'd do just that. He'd been on the receiving end of her flaring temper more than once. Bea would chew Donnie up and spit him out like a piece of gum. "What's he done now?"

"He's been dissecting the pumpkins again," she huffed, narrowing her eyes as she craned her neck to peer around him. Every time she moved, Joe moved. He desperately wanted to laugh, but Bea's menacing glare kept him from giving in to the urge.

"He's just curious, Bea. You know how excited he is about learning medicine. He wants to be a doctor, so he can help people." Joe gave her what he hoped was his most charming smile. Her scowl deepened. Apparently, his most charming wasn't charming enough.

"If he thinks that's helping, he's got another think coming. And you! You really think those puppy eyes are gonna work on me after all these years?"

Joe smiled hopefully. "Yes?" No. With a sigh, he let his head hang low. "You're right. It's my fault. I'm too soft on him." He heard a few chuckles from around the room and knew everyone was waiting to see whether Bea would give in or Joe would end up flat on his face.

Mumbling a few unintelligible words under her breath, Bea stalked back into the kitchen. A light round of applause broke out in celebration of his victory, and Joe bowed with all the grace and grandeur of a Shakespearian actor.

"Thank you, thank you. You are too kind, my lords and ladies." He straightened and spun around to the cowering young man, donning his best Groucho impression. "I got a good mind to join a club and beat you over the head with it."

Donnie snickered, the tension seeming to ease from his boney shoulders. The kid always did like his Groucho impressions.

Being an only child, Joe learned from an early age to rely on his overactive imagination to keep him company on the days his parents were out working hard to earn a decent living—which meant Joe had been pretty much alone most of the time, but he'd been too busy to let the loneliness settle in, what with all the castles to conquer, jungles to explore, and cattle to round up. While most of his school friends were throwing pixelated barrels at big pixelated monkeys, Joe was building forts and labyrinths with the couch cushions and bedsheets.

Living in his own head had been such a part of his existence, when Joe grew up, he had trouble keeping his thoughts in there. Most people figured he had a few screws loose, but he didn't mind. Sure, sometimes he felt a little embarrassed after getting caught having a rather animated conversation with himself, but never ashamed. It was just the way he was.

"I'm sorry, Joe. I didn't mean to cause any trouble," Donnie muttered. His bottom lip jutted out as he stared at the floor, kicking up imaginary dust. Wow, the kid was good.

"Say, that's my bit. Go on, get back to work. And stop dissecting our groceries or you're gonna be getting an early lesson on broken bones from Bea. Elsie will be here soon, anyway."

At the mere mention of the young woman's name, Donnie's cheeks went pink and he shot back into the kitchen. Elsie was part of their motley trio, also eighteen and just as lanky as Donnie. She was a sweetheart and loved to fuss over Joe as much as Bea did. Donnie was goofy over her and everyone knew it; they were just waiting for Donnie to finish locating his backbone.

Someone called Joe's name in a singsong voice, and he turned to Miss Rotherford, bowing politely at her table. Before he could open his mouth, she sprang out of her seat and flung her arms around him, squeezing the air out of his lungs.

"That was the best pie I've ever tasted! And your shop is amazing! I'm having a little shindig in a few weeks, and I was hoping I could pay you to make some of your delicious pies. Everyone will just die!"

"I hope not," Joe gasped in mock horror. "I'd never get any return customers."

She giggled and slapped his arm playfully. "Oh, I knew you could bake, but I had no idea you were so charming." Her boyfriend paid the bill before he helped her into her coat, still smiling brightly. "So, do you think you could whip up five of each pie for me?"

"Five of—" Joe choked. "That's ninety pies!" He had expected a dozen or so, maybe even two dozen. His mind quickly went through the practicalities of it, thinking about how long he'd have to get the extra ingredients, the added expense, and how he would have to ask Elsie and Donnie to put in some extra hours. Sensing his hesitation, she opened her tiny purse and took out bill after bill, shoving them into his hand. It was more money than what twice that number of pies would cost, and he quickly attempted to give some of it back. The more he put back into her little purse, the more she shoved into his hand.

"Oh, no, please, Miss Rotherford, that's not necessary…," he began when Bea materialized like a ghoul from the mist. While his heart slowed to a more nonapoplectic pace, Bea took the money from his hands and stuffed it into her apron pocket, smiling brightly at the couple—which was more frightening than her ghostly reappearing act.

"Don't you worry, Miss Rotherford. Joe's just a little shy. Of course we'll make those pies for you. Your party will be the talk of the town."

"Fantastic! I can't wait. I'll have my assistant call with all the details. I'm going to have to keep everything locked up. If Father finds out, there won't be anything left by the time the guests arrive! Thank you so much." She squeezed Joe's hands, and before a single word could escape his gaping mouth, they were gone. Elsie skipped in just as the couple left. His expression must have said it all, because she looked about ready to turn and make a run for it.

"Is everything all right?" She looked from him to Bea with big brown eyes.

"Fine," Joe replied through his wide grin and gritted teeth. "Would you mind helping Donnie see to the shop? I need a word with Bea." He turned to the iron maiden and bowed regally, motioning toward the kitchen. "After you, your majesty."

Bea said nothing as she marched into the kitchen with Joe following quietly behind. Once they reached the back storage room, like a gunslinger from the Old West, Bea drew first.

"Don't even think about it. I know why you were trying to turn down that job." She pinned him with a stare that could quake Hades itself, but Joe wasn't about to back down. Of course, Bea had no intention of letting him get a word in edgewise until she said her piece.

"And don't you give me any baloney about not enough ovens or ingredients or whatnot. You were gonna say no 'cause that's the biggest order we've had yet, and you're afraid it won't be up to snuff for all them rich folks. That's a load of nonsense and you know it. You saw that girl's face. She loves your pie. Her daddy loves your pie. What's more, his whole office loves your pies. So, you're gonna make those pies, same as you always do, everyone'll love them, and soon you'll need to hire more help because you don't pay me enough to look after the place, cook, clean, babysit you and them two kids, and I swear if that boy keeps dissecting my pumpkins, I'm gonna knock him into next week!" She took a deep breath and released it slowly. "I'm done."

Damn. "Apparently, so am I," he muttered. Once again, she'd fired first and hit him dead between the eyes. He never stood a chance.

"That's what I thought." Bea's expression softened, and she brought Joe into a hearty embrace that left him struggling for breath. Sometimes—most of the time—it drove him nuts. But he knew everything she did was out of concern for him, so he couldn't be too hard on her.

"Joe, you're a good man. What's wrong with letting anyone else besides me and the kids know it too, huh? How else are you gonna find yourself a nice man?"

"Oh no," Joe groaned, shaking his head and gently pushing away from her. "We are not having the 'you need a good man to take care of you' conversation again, and we're certainly not going to have it in the kitchen. I'm a grown man, Bea. I can take care of myself just fine. You don't see me trying to fix you up with every old codger that walks in here."

"Well, maybe you should." An unsavory twinkle came into her lively eyes, making Joe take an instinctive step back. "I could use a good man to keep me warm at night, rubbing my feet, getting cozy…."

“Oh, dear God. Stop, please.” Joe shuddered at the images that stampeded into his head. Thankfully, they fled when Bea whacked him in the arm.

“Don’t be such a prude. That’s probably why you ain’t got no man keeping you warm. Lord knows enough of them try.”

Unfortunately, that was also true. On a daily basis there were plenty of guys dropping subtle hints, and some not so subtle. He supposed it had something to do with that age-old expression about the way to a man’s heart being through his stomach. As much as he wouldn’t mind having someone to keep him warm—as Bea put it—he just couldn’t find it in him to accept any offers, or even flirt back. The fear of losing what had taken him so long to rebuild was too great. He’d tried once. Thought he’d found his happily ever after. It had cost him dearly. He wouldn’t take that chance again. His heart couldn’t take it.

“Joe, you’re a good-looking man, what with all that pretty blond hair and those gorgeous eyes. Like the ocean, that one man said, remember? Not to mention strong and strapping. Plus, you have a mighty fine ass.”

Joe’s eyes widened, and he scrambled to cover his ass with his apron. “Please tell me you don’t go around looking at my butt, because I think I just might be sick. And don’t call my hair pretty. Men don’t have pretty hair. You wouldn’t tell Russell Crowe he’s got pretty hair.” Then again, this was Bea they were talking about. Her eyes lit up, and Joe backed away slowly.

“Oh, now there’s some meat you can sink your teeth into.”

Joe studied the apron in his hands, and nodded absently as Bea prattled on about the handsome actor.

Wrapping the two sashes around his neck, he slowly pulled on the ends.

"He's about your age, isn't he? Thirty-three or somethin'?"

"I don't know how old he is," Joe replied casually, still pulling on the sashes. "I'm thirty-eight. Thank you for remembering." Then again, she *had* written "Congratulations on turning 40!" on his birthday cake a few months ago. He'd initially believed she meant it as a cruel joke. Now he wasn't so sure.

Bea laughed and patted his back so heartily it almost sent him staggering. "I'm just pullin' your leg, Joe. Of course I know how old you are. If you start thinking I'm going senile, I'm gonna whack you one."

Joe let out an indelicate snort. "Like you need an excuse."

Taking the sashes from him, she unwound them from his neck, shaking her head in amusement. "I'm just saying, honey. You're quite a catch, and they know it. It's about time you knew it too. Not everyone's gonna be like that jackass, Blake. Hell, his name alone should have been enough to warn you off."

Joe cringed. "I thought we decided never to speak of him again?" He was *not* going to think about Blake. Goddammit, now he was thinking about Blake. Bea wrapped him back up in her embrace, petting his hair, and he let out a resigned sigh. Arguing with Bea was like stepping in quicksand. The more you struggled, the quicker you sank.

"You can't let him ruin your chances of being happy, Joe. Don't spend your life alone because of that ass. He didn't deserve you."

"I'm not alone," Joe said with a smile. He rubbed his face against Bea's shoulder, purring like a cat. "I got you, and I already know how you feel about my butt." He pulled away and dodged another smack, laughing as he ran back out into the safety of his shop.

"Everything okay?" Donnie asked, his brows drawn together in concern.

"Yeah." Joe grinned and leaned over, whispering loud enough for most of the place to hear. "Keep an eye on your butt. Bea's on the prowl."

The look of sheer terror that crossed Donnie's face was too much, and Joe doubled over with laughter. Bea came out to see what all the fuss was about, and when Joe couldn't answer on account of being too busy guffawing, she looked over at Donnie. The kid flew from the room like it was on fire, and Joe ended up leaning on the counter for support. The rest of the place erupted into laughter, and Bea looked around as if everyone had just lost their marbles. Maybe they had. Joe had that sort of effect on people.

"**WELL,** that was some mighty fine work, partners." Joe waved good-bye to the last customer before turning the shop's sign around to declare the end of another good day. "Donnie, bring the garbage around, will you?"

"Sure thing."

Joe headed to the front door beyond the counter, and a few minutes later, Donnie returned dragging two large black bags behind him. He really needed to start feeding the kid some more meat and potatoes. The squirt couldn't lift a dust bunny. Joe grabbed the bags from him and carried them the rest of the way to the front door and outside onto the sidewalk. Once inside, he locked the front door and headed for the side door to check on the garden between his shop and the fancy shoe boutique next door. It was a strange spot for a memorial garden. Decades ago, before the boutique was a boutique, it was a fancy hat shop owned by Mrs. Lowe. Although the shop had been sold long ago, Mrs. Lowe still owned the building, along with the garden she had made in honor of her late father, who'd died during World War II. Although there was an iron gate at the front that remained closed, as well as one at the back, sometimes kids would sneak in to make out or get up to things they shouldn't be getting up to, so Mrs. Lowe asked Joe to keep an eye on it for her since getting around had become difficult after her hip replacement. Joe didn't mind. When he needed a little break he would sit out here on the stone bench and just enjoy the trees and flowers. It was also where his fire escape was.

They had been busy from open until close, and thanks to Bea, they'd gotten the Rotherford order. The more he thought about it, the more excited he became. He'd never catered a party before. If it was a success, he might have to listen to Bea and think about hiring more help. If things went really well, there was plenty of room in the back kitchen for an extra oven or two, and if he sacrificed some of his savings, he'd be able to manage without too much damage to his finances. It wouldn't be anything fancy, but a bit more space, new furniture, more staff….

The question was, could he do it? He'd thought about having a bigger place once, with a bakery inside. That had been before everything had fallen apart, including him. His business had been steadily growing over the years, and with the economy being what it was, more people than ever needed somewhere affordable to eat, and Joe's shop fit the bill.

Jesus, what the hell was he thinking? His shop had barely changed in fifteen years. He was nearly forty. Was he really going to start taking such risks now?

Outside in the garden he noticed the place was a whole lot darker than usual. The black iron stairs leading up to his apartment were shrouded in shadows thanks to the burned-out bulb underneath it. Great.

"Donnie, grab me a bulb and the ladder, please. Damn wiring's blown out the lights again." He heard Donnie's "okay" and went to check the gate to make sure it was still secure. He picked up a few pieces of stray litter, grumbling to himself. This was the third time in two weeks he'd had to replace the damn bulbs.

Seconds later, Donnie scurried out and set the ladder in place for him. "I thought Pete fixed it?"

"Me too." Seemed every time Pete fixed one thing, another broke. Joe handed the litter to Donnie and was about to climb up the ladder when he heard a low wheezing sound. He froze. "Did you hear that?"

Donnie listened, then shook his head, but Joe had definitely heard something. He stared down at the damp ground and listened. This time the sound was louder, coming from the shadows farther down the garden. He glanced over at Donnie, and the kid's bulging eyes told him he'd heard it too. Making quick work of changing the bulb, Joe swore under his breath. The light didn't quite extend to the far end, but there was enough illumination between it and the moon where he could just about make out various shapes through the shrubbery.

"What do you think it is?" Donnie whispered.

Joe rolled his eyes as Donnie's breath tickled the back of his neck. "You get any closer and you'll be piggyback riding."

"Sorry," Donnie said sheepishly, backing away.

"It's probably just a cat." *Please let it be a cat and not a couple of horny teens getting it on.* Joe slowly edged toward the darkness with Donnie once again breathing down his neck, though Joe imagined the kid's bout of courage had more to do with Elsie watching from the doorway rather than any desire for derring-do. He listened closely for more sounds, but aside from those of the city and Donnie's breathing, he heard nothing. Then he saw it: a big, dark lump on the ground, highlighted by the soft glow of the moon. Whatever it was, it was moving. Just about. "Jesus, it's a person."

"Maybe we should leave him, Joe. It's probably just some homeless guy who's had too much to drink."

"That's no better. We can't just leave some passed-out drunk in Mrs. Lowe's garden." Joe carefully inched closer until he stood over the figure curled up into a tight ball. "Expensive-looking leather jacket for a homeless guy. I don't know about you, but I haven't seen a lot of homeless walking around in leather biker boots, either." He crouched down and shifted one side of the man's black jacket. "Designer too."

"Joe, look!" Donnie pointed to the stained grass just under the man's head.

"Damn, is that what I think it is?" Joe carefully turned the guy's head, finding the black hair at the back matted with blood. "Looks like someone got him good. We need to call an ambulance."

Donnie hesitated before his instincts kicked in, and then he checked for breathing and signs of a pulse. "His breathing's shallow, but he's alive. He's probably got a concussion, so it's not good for him to be out."

"I don't know anything about head wounds other than the kind Bea gives me, and luckily, they're not enough to get me concussed. Not yet, anyway."

"If he's got a concussion and he's out, it could damage his brain. Problem is, we don't know how long he's been out for. We should—"

The man shot out his hand and grabbed a hold of Joe's wrist, causing Donnie to shriek and Joe to nearly jump out of his skin. "Sweet Jesus!" Joe was about to tell Donnie to run and call an ambulance when he realized the injured man was trying to talk. "It's okay. We're going to get you to a hospital, just hang on."

The man made a noise that sounded an awful lot like "no," but that couldn't be right. Maybe the poor bastard was out of his head. Joe leaned in when the guy lifted his head. "No cops," he slurred, tightening his grip on Joe's arm, his voice so low and gravelly Joe wouldn't have heard him if he hadn't been so close. "No hospital."

"What?" Joe shook his head and did his best to remain calm. "Listen, buddy, someone knocked you over the head. You need medical attention."

"Please, no cops. Help me."

"I'm trying to help, but the best I can do is get you to a hospital. I'm not a doctor."

"They'll… kill me. Cops… dead.… No hospital. Please." With that, the guy collapsed back onto the ground.

Well, those were certainly words he didn't care to hear in the same sentence.

Chapter Two

"JOE, we have to get him upstairs," Donnie suggested gravely.

Even if Joe *was* in the habit of bringing mysterious men home to his apartment—which he wasn't—they would at least be conscious, and not possible murderers or criminals. There was a reason this man didn't want them to alert the cops, and that was hardly a good sign. Yet the genuine fear he'd seen in those gray eyes had rattled Joe.

"Even if that wasn't completely insane, you got a crane stashed somewhere I don't know about? Because that's what it's gonna to take to move this guy," Joe hissed.

Donnie gave a very helpful shrug. "You're a big guy."

Technically, a poodle was big to Donnie. "Yeah, and he's bigger. *Much* bigger. Look at him!" Joe wasn't about to point out that he'd be the one shouldering most of the weight. The man's shoes probably weighed more than Donnie did. There was no way Joe could carry this guy up all those stairs by himself. Not without pulling something.

"Stop being such a delicate flower," Bea growled, and Joe nearly keeled over. How in the hell did she do that? *Why* did she do that? Despite the circumstances, Joe couldn't help batting his lashes.

"But I am a delicate flower." That earned him an uninspired expression. "You know, one day I might just wake up and realize I'm the boss around here."

"Yeah, well, when that day comes, you let me know. Now, if we all pitch in, we'll get this guy upstairs. Personally, I think we should just call the cops and let them deal with him."

"We can't. What if he ends up dead and it's our fault because we turned him in?" Donnie said with surprising confidence. "If we just get him upstairs and wake him up, we can find out what this is all about. The longer he's out, Joe, the more damage his head could suffer. We can just call Jules afterward."

Jules was a good friend and an even better nurse. She would know what to do. What was he thinking? This was crazy. Who knew what or who this man was? Despite all his misgivings, Joe found himself grunting in agreement and walking around to hook his arms under those of their new friend. Donnie grabbed a leg, Elsie the other, and Bea the middle. On the count of three, they lifted, and as quickly as they could manage, they carried him carefully up the iron steps toward Joe's apartment, with Joe bearing most of the weight—as expected.

"What's this guy eat for breakfast? Bricks?" Donnie groaned.

It certainly would explain why he was so damned heavy. Even with everyone pitching in, Joe's muscles strained. He picked up the pace so they could reach his apartment before his back gave out. Finally, they managed to get into the living room, where they sat the guy on the couch before they collapsed onto the floor and various furnishings. After catching his breath, Joe stood and walked over to their unconscious guest.

"Elsie, please grab me some warm water and a couple of towels so he doesn't bleed on the couch. Donnie, help me get his jacket off."

They got busy swiftly removing the man's jacket and boots in an attempt to make him more comfortable. From the looks of things, the clothes were all high quality. The charcoal-gray long-sleeved tee stretched over firm muscles and a flat stomach, and his dark jeans fit snug on strong thighs and long legs. Whoever the man was, he certainly wasn't just some bum. Joe searched every pocket in the hopes of finding a wallet, some identification, a business card, cell phone, something that might give them a clue as to who their guest was.

"Did you find anything?" Elsie asked, bringing over the bowl of warm water.

"Nothing. Just some dirt. Donnie, get on the phone to Jules. Ask her what's the earliest she can come by and what we should do in the meantime. Elsie, hold that bowl for me, will you? I'm going to try and get some of this blood off. Bea, could you finish up downstairs?"

Bea gaped like he'd grown three heads. "You want me to just leave you up here with him? What if he wakes up and attacks you? What if he's a murderer? He might be an assassin hired to take you out!"

"What? Don't be ridiculous. No one's been hired to take me out. I bake pies, Bea. I'm not the political head of a foreign territory. I'll be fine."

Bea looked like she was about to argue some more, but thankfully she also knew when Joe meant business, and so she retreated downstairs. Donnie went off to call Jules, and in the meantime, Joe carefully began to clean away as much blood as he could. Soon, he found the source of it: a thin line about two inches long on the side of the man's scalp. It didn't need stitches, but there was one hell of a bump on his noggin. Joe carefully laid him back against the faded brown couch before looking him over.

The guy was younger than Joe had thought, but it was hard to guess how old he was since he was looking a bit scruffy at the moment, what with his hair all over the place and the dark beard, though there were a few gray hairs starting to grow in. There was a nick on his lip, along with several cuts and scrapes around his face, neck, and arms. *Damn.* The guy's knuckles were scraped and bruised. He'd clearly gotten into a pretty bad fight recently.

Donnie came scurrying back from the kitchen, his chest heaving as if he'd run a lap rather than the few feet it was. "Jules says we need to wake him up and get him to talk. Keep an eye on him in case he's sick or dizzy, and keep him awake for a few hours. See about convincing him to get to a hospital. He needs to be observed overnight. She says she's sorry, but she's working tonight. She'll try to come by as soon as she can."

"Okay." Joe ran his fingers through his hair as he thought about his next move.

Donnie took a seat beside Elsie, both watching him anxiously. "What are we gonna do, Joe?"

As sure as Joe was that the guy hadn't been hired to assassinate him, he didn't know if the man was dangerous. Not to mention his last words hadn't exactly filled Joe with warm fuzzy feelings. "Why don't you kids go help Bea? I'll let you know when he's awake, or if I need anything."

Donnie opened his mouth but caught Joe's subtle nod toward Elsie, who looked a little pale. The kid quickly jumped to his feet and took her hand. "Come on, Elsie. Let's go help Bea." Elsie gazed up at Donnie like he was her knight in shining armor and followed him, smiling, out of the apartment.

"All right, Joe, you can do this." Inhaling deeply, Joe crouched in front of the unconscious man and pinched his hand lightly. "Hey. Wake up."

Nothing happened.

"Of course nothing happened." What did he think would happen with a pinch like that? If Bea had been here, she'd have told him off for it, or more likely, probably given him a tweak that put his own to shame. Bracing himself, he pinched the man's hand. Hard.

Nothing.

"Aw, come on, man. Do me a favor, already. I nearly pulled something dragging your butt up here. The least you could do is be conscious." He pinched the guy again. "Wake up!" Another harsh pinch later, the guy groaned. *Now we're getting somewhere.*

Gently shaking the guy's shoulder with one hand and patting the man's cheek with the other, Joe was about to smack him one more time when the guy popped up like a jack-in-the-box.

Joe forgave himself for the inelegant yelp that escaped him. He hit the carpet with a painful *thud. What just happened?*

Managing to suck some air into his lungs, when the man landed on him, Joe did his best not to panic by shutting his eyes tight and remaining perfectly still. Then he remembered the heavy weight pinning him down wasn't a bear and therefore most likely not fooled by his playing possum. Were bears fooled by that kind of thing? Maybe this wasn't the best time to ponder that. The weight shifted, and before Joe knew it, there was a forearm pressed against his neck. Suddenly, this all seemed like a very bad idea. Actually, *bad* was an understatement. He could just about hear Bea's "I told you so." He hated when she told him so.

"Who do you work for," the man demanded, his face red and his steel gaze pinning Joe to the spot. "Answer me!"

Joe shook his head as best he could. "No one! Me! I work for me. I bake pies."

The man narrowed his eyes. "Who are you?"

"I'm not going to hurt you," Joe said, his hands up at his sides to show he didn't intend to pull anything funny. He hadn't exactly thought about what he'd do once the guy woke up. *Smart, Joe. Very smart.*

It wasn't like he was a weakling. He was six feet tall, after all, and though not overly muscular, still strong enough. Of course, the man above him was big and solid, at least twenty to thirty pounds heavier than Joe, with an added three to four inches in height. From the feel of hard thigh muscles pressed firmly against Joe's ribs, the broadness of his chest, the strength in his arms, and a look that said "try it and I'll throw you across the room without breaking a sweat," Joe realized he might have bitten off a little more than he could chew. His best option would be to reason with the man. If all else failed, well, then, he would simply have to punch the guy and hope for the best.

"My friends and I found you in the garden downstairs, just outside my shop. Remember? You went unconscious, so I was trying to wake you up. You might have a concussion." Joe hoped his smile didn't look as shaky as it felt.

The man moved his free hand to the back of his head and winced. Well, at least he knew Joe hadn't been lying about that.

"I'm Joe. And you are…?"

"I…." The man's dark brows drew together. He seemed to genuinely struggle with a reply. For a moment Joe thought maybe the guy was trying to bide himself some time to come up with some bull story, but when he turned his gaze back to Joe, Joe was stunned to see the panic there. "I—oh God, I don't know."

Just when he thought things couldn't get any stranger.

The man jumped to his feet and backed up as he frantically looked around the room. "Where the hell am I? Why can't I remember anything?" Spotting the window, he rushed over to it and squinted out into the dark streets. "What city is this?"

Joe gradually stood, not wanting to make any sudden movements. "You're in my apartment, above my shop in Manhattan. New York City." He felt a pang in his chest as the guy went frightfully still.

"New York? Am I supposed to be in New York? I can't remember anything before… before now." He closed his eyes tight and gritted his teeth. It was obvious he was racking his brain for whatever information might be in there. Joe wished there was something he could do, but it was out of his hands. It wasn't as if he could offer any help. He'd never seen the man before tonight.

"Let's take things slow," Joe said reassuringly. "You were out for a good while, and I'm guessing the nasty bump on your head has something to do with why you're having trouble remembering. I'm sure it'll come back to you. You just have to take it easy." He motioned to the couch. "Come on. Sit down. You're safe here."

The man eyed him warily. "I'm fine standing."

"Okay. My name is Joe Applin. I own the pie and coffee shop downstairs. I brought you up here because you needed help and you refused to go to a hospital."

Something seemed to have occurred to the guy because he marched over to Joe, his menacing growl giving Joe a start. "Did you call the cops?"

Joe took a step back. "What? No. You said no cops." Was it possible the guy couldn't remember? Joe didn't have a clue about this sort of thing other than what he saw in Hollywood. Amnesia? Really? This whole situation was like something out of one of Bea's Lifetime movies. Joe couldn't help his skepticism. "Listen, why don't you rest for a bit? Don't overdo it. My friend's a nurse, but she's at work at the moment. Are you feeling sick at all or dizzy?" The guy shook his head and Joe breathed a sigh of relief. "Okay, then. Well, she said I need to keep you up for a while, and if you go to sleep, you need to be observed. We'll see what she has to say when she gets here and take it from there, okay?"

"Why would you help me?" The man took a step closer. Joe instinctively did the same before taking a step in the opposite direction. The guy sure had an imposing way about him, one that had Joe ready to bolt. It would be wise not to underestimate his guest. Lack of memory didn't mean the man was incapable of who knew what. Maybe he wasn't thinking this through enough.

"Why wouldn't I?"

"You expect me to believe you brought me up here out of the goodness of your heart?" Something dangerous flashed in the man's silver eyes. Before Joe had a chance to figure out what it was, the guy threw a hand out and grabbed Joe's arm. He jerked Joe hard against him. "Maybe you brought me up here for something else." His eyes dropped to Joe's lips before moving back up. "I don't have any money. Were you hoping I'd repay you some other way?"

The realization of what the guy was saying boiled Joe's blood, and he shoved the stranger away from him. Of all the nerve! "Are you kidding me? I drag your heavy ass up here, welcome you into my home, and you accuse me of trying to take advantage of you?"

The man narrowed his eyes again, his head cocked to one side as he studied Joe. "Why else would you help me? What's your motive?"

"Motive? Who are you? Columbo? How about to help a fellow human being? I know it's hard for you to trust anyone right now, so I'm going to ignore your insult, but you're lucky I'm the one who found you because I'm probably the only one dumb enough to listen to you when you said no cops. I sell pies. I'm not an evil mastermind." He motioned around him to his small but cozy apartment. "This isn't exactly Meteora."

The man arched an eyebrow. "*For Your Eyes Only*?"

Joe threw his hands up. "Oh, *that* you know? Great. I feel much better now. That'll come in handy during our James Bond marathon."

"All right, I get it. I'm sorry." Once again, Joe found himself under the man's scrutiny, and it made him feel uncomfortable. It was as if the guy was mentally taking note of every hair out of place on Joe's head or each tiny wrinkle in his pants. "Where's your remote control Lotus Esprit Turbo?"

Joe felt the heat rising in his cheeks, and he suddenly found it difficult to keep his gaze in one spot, especially on the grumpy—not to mention astute—mystery man standing across from him.

"Holy hell, you *have* one?" The guy let out a laugh.

"Maybe." Joe crossed his arms over his chest, and glared at whatever-his-name-was. That's what he got for helping a guy out. "It was autographed by Roger Moore and auctioned off for charity," Joe replied with a sniff. "Besides, it's not like I play with it." Why the hell was he explaining himself to a guy he'd found facedown in the dirt? His expression must have said as much, because the laughing stopped.

"You're right. I'm sorry. Here you are helping me, and I'm being a jerk." The gentle words got Joe's attention, and he found himself caught off guard by the man's arresting smile. It was certainly a far cry from his previous menacing growls. It was like the guy had two personalities. Oh God, what if the guy *had* two personalities? "I think it's kind of sweet, actually."

"Now you're just messing with me."

"No, I'm not. I really do think it's sweet. Then again, you seem like that kind of guy. I apologize for insulting you earlier. I don't come across guys like you often."

If it hadn't been for the completely open and honest expression, Joe would have thought the guy was trying to pull one over on him. "How do you know?"

"I don't know. Gut feeling. Feels like I should listen to it."

"Okay, well, there's not much we can do until Jules has a look at you. Unless, uh… well, I suppose you can still go to the hospital. I could call a taxi and take you down there." Was it too much to hope for?

"Not going to happen." There was no hesitation in his reply, and the light in those bright silver eyes dimmed. "No cops, no hospital. I know it sounds crazy, but all I know is that it's really important they don't know I'm here. If I go there, I don't know what'll happen to me." He took a step toward Joe, his expression softening as he pleaded. "I promise to behave myself. I know you have no reason to trust me or keep helping me, but… just give me a little time. At least until something comes to me. Please. Whatever's going on, I know if I go out there without knowing who or what's after me… I'm not going to last. I *need* to remember."

Wow. Not ominous at all. "I don't know." Joe rubbed his hands over his face as he paced the living room. This was crazy. Helping the guy out one night was one thing, but letting him stay here until he recovered his memory? What if it didn't happen? What if he was lying? Joe felt like a jerk for saying it, but he had to think about Bea, Donnie, and Elsie. Not to mention his customers. The last thing he wanted was for someone to get hurt because of him.

"I want to help you, I really do, but if you're right and someone out there is trying to hurt you, how do I know they won't come after me and my friends? I can't let you, or anyone else, put them in danger." He hated how the man deflated before him, but it was the right thing to do, wasn't it? Maybe it would convince his new friend to speak to the proper authorities.

"I understand. You've done plenty for me already, and I'm grateful for that." The guy walked over to the couch and sat to put on his boots before picking up his jacket and searching his pockets. He gave Joe a sincere smile that reached his eyes. He didn't seem upset or even irritated that Joe was casting him out. "Thanks. I've gotten this far, right? I'll be fine." His expression turned to one of embarrassment. "I feel like a real jackass asking, but could you maybe spare a few dollars for something to eat? Looks like my memory isn't the only thing missing."

Oh for crying out loud. Before Joe could put any rational thought into it, he nodded. "Stay." What was he doing? Was he nuts? He didn't know the first thing about this man. The circumstances of how and where Joe had found him should've been enough for him to walk away from this mess. Actually, the mention of "dead" should have had Joe speed-dialing the cops, but something about the guy, the genuine look of vulnerability and distress, had all of Joe's wires crossed.

"Really, Joe, it's okay. You're right. If I'm in danger, it's possible I might bring that down on you." He looked down at his knuckles and sighed. "From the looks of it, I can handle myself in a fight."

"Yeah, because that worked so well the last time," Joe muttered. "Look, it's fine. All I ask is that you stay up here. No wandering outside or downstairs. Not until we know a little more about what's going on. Deal?" Maybe if he kept his new friend out of sight for a while, they'd figure something out.

"Really?"

"Yes." Joe held his hand out. "Have we got a deal?"

Joe stood stock-still as strong, muscular arms squeezed him tight. That, along with the feel of the guy's breath against his skin, sent an unexpected tingle through Joe's body. His new friend pulled away, his timid smile catching Joe off guard.

"Sorry. I didn't mean to get all touchy-feely on you. I'm just really grateful." He headed back to the couch and the warmth Joe felt went with him. "Are you all right?"

Joe looked at him blankly. "Huh?"

"You were humming something, and you got this sort of faraway look in your eyes." Despite the concern in his voice, the guy looked rather amused.

"Oh uh…." *Fudgebunnies! It's a little early for him to find out you're a nutcase, Joe. Keep it together.* "Sorry, my mind just wandered. It does that a lot. Don't worry about earlier. Say, uh, we should probably think of what to call you, until you can remember your name."

"Any suggestions?"

"Me?" Joe looked him over. Tall, handsome, rugged, thick biceps, and a nice full bottom lip. A name suddenly popped into his mind, making him smile. "Chris. Like that actor. You kinda look like him. Darker hair, though, and uh, not Australian." He motioned to his bicep. "It's the arms." Wait, did he just say that? Now that he thought about it…. He cocked his head to one side and frowned. "Except you don't look like a *Chris*. You look more like a Tom. Yeah, I like that better."

"Um, okay. I remind you of Chris but look like a Tom. Tom it is, then." *Tom* let out a husky laugh. He looked amused.

What had he gotten himself into? Joe felt himself grinning like an idiot. "All right, Tom. You sit tight and stay awake. I'm going to go downstairs to check on Bea and the kids, then I'll get you something to eat, if you think your stomach's up to it." He'd started toward the door when Tom called out to him.

"I hate to be a pain, because you've done so much for me already, but can I ask a favor?"

"Sure."

"Would you mind if I shaved, maybe had a shower? I don't like looking like I just crawled out of the gutter. Even if that's sort of what I did."

At least Tom had a sense of humor.

"Right. Sorry, with everything going on, it slipped my mind to offer." Joe crossed the living room into the hall to the small closet. He grabbed a couple of towels and tossed them at Tom on his way to the bedroom. He returned with a pair of pajama bottoms and the loosest T-shirt he owned. "Here you go. I'll see about getting your clothes washed. We're roughly the same size. Except for the shirt." He motioned the span of his own far less muscular chest. "That's the biggest size T-shirt I own, so it should fit."

"Are you sure it's okay for me to stay?" Tom asked, looking uncertain.

"Positive." Joe went back into his room unable to understand why he was being so accommodating. *You keep telling yourself that, Joe.* He promptly told himself to shut it and pulled out a warm blanket and fluffy pillow. Walking back out into the living room, Joe set the bedding on the couch. "There you go. I'll be back in a few minutes, after I check on the shop and send everyone home."

"Okay." Tom beamed. The guy really had one hell of a smile. It was hard to associate that with the evidence of violence marking the man's skin. "And thanks again. This is really decent of you."

"Don't mention it."

To think this day started like any other. This morning had been like any other morning, this afternoon like any other afternoon, and now? Now he had a tall, dark, handsome stranger in his bathroom, wearing his pajamas. Under normal circumstances, that alone would have been cause to celebrate. Except these weren't normal circumstances, and Tom wasn't upstairs on account of Joe taking him up on his flirting. As if a good-looking guy like Tom would even flirt with someone like him. Not that he was interested or anything, he was just—Joe didn't get a chance to finish the thought. The moment he stepped foot into the empty café, he was ambushed.

"So who is he?" Donnie asked, trembling with anticipation.

Definitely time to cut back on the kid's caffeine intake.

"Ah, now there's the question we all want to know the answer to," Joe replied, looking around the shop, happy to see everything was in tip-top shape and ready for the next day. Not that he had expected any less from his motley crew. He could always count on them to man the ship while he was away. Beside him, Elsie wrung her hands nervously.

"He didn't tell you?" Elsie asked him.

"He didn't know." Joe sighed and leaned against the door.

The three exchanged glances before Bea peered at him. "What do you mean he didn't know? Didn't know what?"

"Anything. Poor guy can't even remember his own name." Joe walked over to one of the two large glass windows and pulled down the heavy canvas shade, securing the small ring over the tiny hook in the wooden frame. "Guess he got whacked a little harder than we thought."

The two youngsters' eyes widened, and it was like he'd walked into some Broadway production. He went to the next window to pull the shade down on that one.

Donnie looked a little too excited for his own good. "You mean… he's got *amnesia*? I read about that."

"Baloney," Bea huffed. "Amnesia's something you see in those old Hollywood movies. It's not real."

"'Course it's real. Wouldn't be a medical condition otherwise." Joe smiled sweetly and pinched Bea's cheek. "What you mean to say, my dearest, is that you think he's full of it."

Bea slapped his hand away, her gaze boring into him as he headed toward the back of the shop. "He's stringing you along, honey, and you're letting him."

Joe waved his hand dismissively, ignoring that last statement. "Listen, don't you fret your pretty little head. Jules will be here as soon as she can, and she'll tell us what's what."

"I tell you, there's something sinister about that boy," Bea insisted.

"That's why you shouldn't watch so many soap operas. This isn't some 'wealthy heiress gets pregnant with the stableboy's baby' scandal. He's just some poor guy who was in the wrong place at the wrong time." Joe remembered the look on Tom's face when he realized he couldn't remember. How could Joe ignore the pain the man was in? "What am I supposed to do, huh? Kick him out? You should have seen his face. He looked so… lost. He's a nice enough guy, I think. I can't shove him back out into the gutter. Where would he go? What if something terrible happens to him?" The thought made him feel sick to his stomach. "I can't picture him ending up sleeping on a bench or some dank alley with rats and fleas, and what if he got sick and—"

"All right already," Bea grumbled. "Geez Louise. Now who's been watching too many dramas? I'll tell you one thing: I'm not going home while he's sleeping a stone's throw away from you. He might knife you in your sleep. Steal your shoes." She stomped over to pick up trusty ole Silver, and Joe released a groan when she came out swinging. "I'm taking first watch."

"You're kidding."

"If Bea's staying to watch over you, so am I," Donnie declared, chest all puffed up like a baby bird. "I'll take second watch."

"I'll take third," Elsie chirped.

Dammit all. This was the last thing he needed right now. As if a sixty-year-old woman and two spindly adolescents would be any match for a guy of Tom's strength. Joe appreciated their concern, but if Tom was dangerous, Joe couldn't allow his friends to put themselves in harm's way. The decision to allow the man to stay in his apartment had been his, and he would deal with the consequences.

Walking up to Bea, he gingerly took the old aluminum baseball bat from her hands, and turned her away from the kids. "Bea, I know you all mean well, but let's be practical about this. You saw the man. As much as I can confidently say Tom—that's what we're calling him by the way—poses no threat, if he did, do you really think Donnie and Elsie would stand a chance?" Bea opened her mouth, but Joe was quick to cut her off. "I promise you, I'll be careful. I need you to keep things running as usual. I'll be a little late downstairs tomorrow since Jules is coming by."

"I don't like it," Bea groused, though he knew she'd do as he asked, so he gave her cheek a kiss.

"Thank you."

"I want to talk to him first," she said stubbornly.

Well, it was the best he could hope for. "Okay. Finish up down here and give me about ten minutes. I don't want everyone barreling upstairs and scaring the life out of him. Try to go easy on the poor guy." Not waiting around for a reply, he sped through the kitchen to the set of stairs at the back that led up to his apartment. If anyone was in danger, it was poor Tom.

Chapter Three

JOE reached his living room only to find it empty, and for a moment he wondered if maybe Tom had decided to go after all.

"Tom?" Joe took a peek down the hall and spotted the light coming out from under the closed bathroom door.

"I'm just finishing up," Tom called out. "Be right out."

Joe couldn't explain why the mere sound of the man's voice caused butterflies to appear in his stomach. He tried not to think about how nice it was to hear his apartment filled with more than the sound of the TV, or no sound at all. Man, he really needed to get out more. He'd been so caught up in his thoughts he didn't hear Tom come out of the bathroom. When he saw movement directly in front of him, Joe gave a start, and his jaw nearly became unhinged. *Oh sweet Betty Crocker.*

Tom stood in the borrowed pajama pants and undershirt—which was pulled snugly across his well-muscled chest. His newly washed hair was charmingly tousled, his chiseled jaw clean-shaven, and his skin naturally tanned, which made his silver eyes stand out all the more. He stood barefoot with a towel around his neck and a big grin stretched across his face. He looked younger, but the little creases at the corners of his eyes and the fine silver hairs subtly woven in with his pitch-black hair said Tom was probably close to Joe's age.

Picking his jaw up off the floor, Joe attempted to regain some form of decorum before Tom ended up thinking worse things about him than him being a little nuts. "There you are. Everything all right?"

"Yeah, thanks. You okay?" Tom cocked his head to one side as he studied Joe.

"Yep, fine. Listen, I hope you won't be offended, but I don't really have much—any, actually—family except for Bea, Elsie, and Donnie who help me run the shop, and they've gotten it in their heads to have a word with you. So, could you maybe humor them for me?"

Tom swept past him, looking back over his shoulder with a smile that was nothing short of sinful. "They trying to protect your virtue?"

Oh my God. Joe sucked in his breath and found himself trailing behind Tom without any thought in his head. Tom settled on the couch, those intense eyes directed at him. Was Tom… flirting with him?

"Uh, yeah. Something like that," Joe muttered, whether to Tom's question or his own, he wasn't certain. Could Tom really be flirting? Nah, he was most likely teasing. Maybe Joe was just hearing what he wanted to. Yep, that's right. Tom wasn't flirting with him at all. He better get a hold of himself before he did something silly, like invite a handsome stranger with amnesia to sleep under the same roof as him. No, wait. He'd already done that.

"Are you sure it's okay for me to stay? I mean, I wouldn't want your girlfriend, or boyfriend getting upset with you." The smile was gone from Tom's face, replaced by a sudden intensity in his eyes. His forwardness was certainly unexpected. Would Tom have second thoughts if Joe said he was gay? Joe didn't hide who he was. He'd spent enough of his youth doing that. He didn't exactly go around waving a neon sign that pointed it out, but he didn't hide it.

"No. No boyfriend to get upset with me," Joe replied, studying Tom's expression. Tom's lips curled into a smile, and Joe found himself liking it. "Will that be a problem?"

"That you don't have a boyfriend? No." Tom's eyes sparkled with mischief. "Or do you mean being gay? That's not a problem for me, Joe. I might not remember who I am, but I know what team I play for." He raked his gaze over Joe and his cheeks went slightly pink before he lowered his eyes to his fingers. "Definitely not a problem. So, there's no one special in your life?" Tom lifted his gaze to meet Joe's.

Come on, Joe. What more do you want the guy to do? Change his online status? Announce it on the radio? Send out a smoke signal? Either way, it didn't matter. Joe knew next to nothing about this man, much less his intentions. He needed to keep his wits about him.

A forceful knock startled them both. Cursing under his breath, Joe let in the chastity brigade. It was probably for the best. He really shouldn't be entertaining any kind of risqué thoughts about Tom. The man's name wasn't even Tom, for heaven's sake!

"Oh my God." Elsie leaned into Joe, whispering hoarsely and loud enough for everyone to hear, including Tom. "He's gorgeous!"

Donnie crossed his arms over his chest with a huff. "He's not that good-looking."

Elsie ignored him and made her way over to Tom, who smiled and seemed a little too amused for his own good. "Hi. I'm Elsie." She narrowed her pretty brown eyes and stood on her toes. "You're not a murderer, are you? Because Joe's like a big brother to us, and if you hurt him, well, Donnie's going to knock you out."

Tom shook his head somberly, though Joe could tell the man was fighting back a chuckle. "I know it's hard to believe, considering I don't remember much of anything, but I think something like that is part of a man's nature. I'm not going to hurt Joe. He's already done more for me than most people would have. I owe him."

"Oh, for crying out loud." Bea faced Elsie and Donnie before jutting a finger toward the door. "You two get going. I expect you bright and early. Joe and I will take care of this drifter."

"But—" Donnie attempted to protest, only to cower at the sight of Bea's formidable eyebrow. "Come on, Elsie. I'll walk you home."

"Nice to meet you, Mr. Tom! Good night, Joe," Elsie said with a cheerful wave.

Tom and Joe waved back before turning their attention to Bea. As soon as the door closed behind the youngsters, she stomped over to Tom with all her usual grace and subtlety, poking him in the shoulder. She opened her mouth to speak, then closed it before peering at him.

"Do I know you?" she asked.

Tom looked hopeful. "I don't know. Do you?"

Was it possible Bea had met Tom before? Joe took a step toward her. "Have you seen him before, Bea?"

Bea looked Tom over, and after what seemed like forever, she shook her head. Both Joe and Tom sighed with disappointment. "Felt like maybe I had, but no. I'd definitely remember you." She tapped the side of her head. "Sharp as ever. Must be the eyes. They remind me of that young fella who was in here this morning with his girl. The one who ordered all the pies."

Now that Joe thought about it, Bea was right. Ms. Rotherford's boyfriend had very similar silver eyes. He was tall with dark hair too. Dammit. For a moment there, he thought they'd caught a break. Seeming to get back to her original train of thought, Bea poked Tom in the shoulder again.

"Now you listen here, young man. That bump on your melon ain't gonna be nothing compared to what I'm gonna do to you if you hurt Joe. You got me?" Tom nodded and took a small step away from Bea—who just took that as an invitation to take one closer. "Joe's a good man, and I don't care how handsome he thinks you are. If you hurt him, you'll have me to deal with."

Surely, Joe hadn't just heard what he thought he'd heard? She hadn't just said….

Tom's eyebrows shot up, and he looked at Joe. "You think I'm handsome?"

Yep, he *had* heard what he thought he'd heard. Because his life wasn't awkward enough. Joe tried to appear as aloof as possible, but the crooked grin on Tom's face wasn't helping any.

"I never said that. I mean, not that you aren't—just that I wasn't—I mean, I'm not saying…." What the hell *was* he saying? He tried to find a way out of the hole

Bea had dug for him, and when he couldn't, he gave up. Not like he hadn't made a fool of himself already. "Never mind." He motioned to Bea with a saccharine curl of his lips. "Please, carry on."

Tom did just that, turning to Bea with a charming smile and leaning over to whisper in her ear. Unlike Elsie, Joe couldn't hear a word of what Tom was saying. Now he was really starting to get nervous.

"You bet," Bea stated, winking at Tom knowingly. Again Tom leaned over to whisper, and Joe found himself leaning in the same direction. When had they started playing Chinese whispers? And why wasn't he being let in on it?

Bea waved a hand dismissively. "He's just shy when it comes to that sort of thing. It's been a while. A really, really long while."

Joe smacked his hand to his head. There was no way on God's green earth this was happening. Had she lost her marbles?

He stalked over to Bea and dragged her into the kitchen before she started giving Tom figures and statistics. "Have you lost your mind? Why did you tell him I thought he was handsome? And please tell me you didn't just tell him what I thought you told him. We talked about this. You remember, right? You remember the man who single-handedly destroyed my life? You have any idea what it's like to end up on the street with nothing? I lost everything Bea, and if it hadn't been for Officer Baker, I could have lost my life. I just can't go through that again."

"What are you talking about? And don't you dare for a second think I don't care about what happens to you Joe Applin. Who took you in and tended to you after what that no good bastard did to you? That man out there isn't Blake. You need to stop beating yourself up for what happened. You did nothing wrong, Joe."

It sure as hell didn't feel that way.

"You need to forgive yourself for what happened and move on with your life. If a man looked at my butt the way Tom was looking at yours when you were talking to Elsie, I'd be enjoying him with a side of ice cream by now."

"Oh my God!" He was going to keel over, he just knew it. He could feel the palpitations in his heart already. Joe paced. He hated pacing. "Where do I begin? The man doesn't even know his own name! Don't you think he has more important things to worry about than whether or not I find him attractive? Doesn't matter how long it's been, which by the way, your estimate of that time frame is highly exaggerated, and just because he's gay doesn't mean he's ready to jump in the sack with me."

"Why not?" Bea blinked, clearly perplexed.

Joe had no idea how else to explain it to Bea. Just because there was a hot gay man in his living room, that did not mean they would automatically end up under the sheets together, and no matter what Bea thought, Joe was *not* a prude. He'd had plenty of experiences with men, both before and after Blake. Maybe he hadn't gotten very far with them, but he wasn't completely inexperienced.

"You could do a lot worse, Joe. If I were you, I'd—"

Slapping his hands over his ears, he spun away from her. "Excuse me for a moment." He went to the oven, pulled open the door, and dropped to his knees.

The kitchen door creaked, and Joe heard Tom's worried voice, sealing the deal. "Everything all right in here?" From the corner of Joe's eye he could see Tom look from Bea to Joe, whose cheek was now resting against one of the oven racks as he felt around for the right knob.

"Don't mind him. He's just being overdramatic again," Bea said with a snort.

"What's he doing?" Tom asked, bemused.

"I'm trying to bake myself." Joe's muffled voice echoed from inside the large appliance. "Would you mind throwing your towel over the radiator in the bathroom? And don't let Bea give my eulogy. God knows what she'll say."

Bea rolled her eyes. "He thinks the world's gonna implode or something just 'cause you figured out he thinks you're handsome."

There was a loud thud as Joe's head hit the roof. "Christ, woman, you trying to finish me off? He didn't figure anything out, because you told him! Could someone direct my hand to the right dial? I'd like to finish this quickly."

"Stop using the Lord's name in vain," Bea reprimanded, smacking his ass with what he could only assume was Tom's towel.

Was there no end to this humiliation? I'm not such a bad guy, Joe thought. I eat my vegetables, respect my elders—Bea doesn't count and you know that, Lord. What will it take? More donations to the orphans? More volunteering at the Y? I'll do it. Just make it stop.

"This from the woman who swears like a drunken sailor after getting one cocktail in her!" Joe heard Tom's husky laugh and groaned as it grew closer. A hand came to rest on his lower back, and he froze. He could feel the heat from Tom's touch even through his layers of clothing. Either that or he had somehow managed to get the oven going. This was bad, very bad.

"Come on out of there, Joe. It's okay."

After some hesitation and a few encouraging murmurs from Tom, Joe carefully sat back on his heels. Perhaps he was being a tad melodramatic. He smoothed down his hair and shirt, muttering embarrassingly, "You're mentally incapacitated, and my friend's trying to set you up on a date."

"Heaven knows you need one," Bea muttered.

Unbelievable. "Someone steal your last pair of panty hose or something? Jesus." Joe let Tom help him to his feet but couldn't quite bring himself to look the man in the eye. There was no doubt in his mind that if Tom could recall his memories, he'd agree this was the craziest thing to ever happen to him. Joe cast Bea a sideward glance. "What happened to sinister? First you wanted to introduce him to Silver, and now you want me to serve him up with a side of ice cream."

What is wrong with you? My God, this is getting worse by the minute. Every time he opened his mouth, strange words came out. Joe swallowed hard and found Tom looking around the room, the corners of his mouth twitching.

Bea opened her mouth—no doubt to reveal more of Joe's nonexistent love life, so he hastily ushered her toward the door. "Thanks, Bea. Now, you run along, and I'll call if I need anything." He got her to the side door leading to the outside stairs, grateful Tom stayed behind in the kitchen. He probably sensed Joe was on the verge of going off like a firecracker.

"I'm telling you, Joe, that man looks at you the way people look at your pies. He wants to take a bite out of you, and I sure do hope you let him."

"That's been my plan this whole time," Joe whispered conspiratorially. "That's why I'm rushing you out, because we're going to sit on the couch like a couple of teenagers and you don't want to be around when the groping starts."

Bea arched an eyebrow. "No one likes a smartass."

"But you love me, I know you do. Good night and thank you." He kissed her cheek and gently shoved her out the door. Once the door was closed, he dropped his head against it with a heavy thud. Thank God, the worst was over.

"They're really nice. A little… odd, but sweet."

"Sweet Jesus!" Joe gave a start and spun away from the door, tripping over his own feet in the process. He was getting to know his carpet pretty well these days. With a groan, he rolled onto his back, his eyes shut tight, mostly because he felt Tom kneel down beside him, and he couldn't find the nerve to face him just yet.

Why was it that when a guy tried his hardest not to look like a complete loon, fate decided to prove that's just what he was? His life used to be so calm and uneventful. Now there was a tall, sinfully handsome man with no name and a magnetic force strong enough to pull in a cruise ship staying with him. Why did Joe get the feeling he was about to enter deep waters? Two words sprang to mind.

Man overboard!

"Joe? Are you all right?"

Tom's voice was laced with genuine concern, and when Joe opened his eyes, Tom's expression was overflowing with it.

"Mm?" was all Joe could muster. He was too enthralled by what he thought he saw to string coherent words together, not to mention Tom's nearness was sending his pulse soaring like a rocket.

"Thank God. Sorry I scared you. You're kind of jumpy, aren't you?"

What was he supposed to say to that? Yes, yes he was. Heat rose to his face. He was blushing, which, thanks to his fair skin and freckles, would be a lot more obvious. Swell. He was grateful when Tom pulled him to his feet.

"Tom, I, um, I should probably warn you. I'm always like this. I'm fidgety, talk to myself, stick my head in ovens and trip over things because when I haven't got my head stuck in an appliance, it's up in the clouds somewhere. I run on coffee, and when the coffee's run out, I still act like I'm running on coffee. Lots and lots of coffee. Even when I'm sitting still, my mind's going at full speed. I'm just telling you this so you don't think you're staying with some crazy twit. I'm not crazy or a twit. I know I probably sound like it right now, but I'm pretty certain Jules would have said something if I was certifiably ready for Bedlam, and if you haven't guessed, I ramble too. Why are you looking at me like that?"

Tom chuckled and led Joe over to the couch, pulling him down with him as he sat. He was grinning from ear to ear, and Joe couldn't figure out what he'd done to be on the receiving end of such a smile. Now that the craziness had somewhat ebbed—or spread—it was too soon to tell—it was a little strange sitting here on his usually empty couch in the middle of his usually empty living room, holding hands with a complete stranger and liking it. Maybe Bea had whacked him a little too hard on the head and *he* was the one lying facedown with a concussion.

"Joe, you don't have to explain yourself, or be anyone other than you. Not for anyone else and certainly not for me."

Joe eyed him skeptically. "Yeah?"

"The way Elsie, Donnie, and Bea jump to your defense, shows how much they care about you. Even if you are a little crazy." Tom laughed softly at Joe's pout, his eyes twinkling with mischief. "Lucky for both of us, I happen to be a guy who doesn't mind a little crazy."

"Ah, but you don't know that," Joe pointed out, tapping Tom lightly on the head. "You might not like it at all."

Tom smiled warmly. "If that's the case, you're well on your way to changing my mind."

"Oh, uh, thanks." Joe looked down at his hands, still in Tom's larger ones. Geez, was he really that pale? Next to Tom, he certainly looked it. Then again, the man was bronzed all over. Maybe he was a bouncer at a nightclub. Joe stifled a gasp. What if Tom was a hustler, one of those playboys who got paid to keep wealthy men… entertained? There wasn't a shortage of naughty nightclubs around here. Then again, Tom wouldn't have been so angry at the thought of Joe possibly wanting Tom to "repay" him for his kindness. Tom chuckled, and Joe snapped out of it. That had to be the worst idea he'd ever come up with. Bea was right. He was overdramatic.

"You're drifting off again."

"Sorry. Started wondering who you might be." Should he pull his hands out of Tom's? This was a little strange. Wasn't it? Yes. Maybe. He discreetly pulled his hand away to scratch a pretend itch on his jaw.

"Conclusion?"

"Uh, you don't want to know."

Tom sat back, his eyes alight with amusement. "Try me."

This should be interesting. "Um, high-end rent boy."

Tom's jaw went slack. "A prostitute?"

Well, when you say it like that, of course it sounds bad. "Which is why I said you didn't want to know."

Tom stared at him before bursting into laughter. "Joe, you are something else."

Joe didn't quite know what to say to that. This was uncharted territory for him, and he was lost in the woods without so much as a matchstick to light his way. Blake had been enough of an experience, thanks very much, and what had it gotten him? A whole lot more than just heartache, that's what. Hadn't he learned his lesson? Joe stood quicker than he should have and backed away from the couch.

"Um, I'm going to grab another blanket for you. Be right back." He spun around and all but sprinted to his room, cursing himself for being such a coward.

No, he wasn't a coward; he was sensible. He had to focus on helping Tom regain his memory and then… then what? Say good-bye, he supposed. He tried not to think about that as he swiftly changed into his own pajamas, then grabbed an extra blanket for Tom, along with some of his own bedding. He went back into the living room, where he found Tom sitting right where he left him, still smiling. The guy sure did smile a lot. Not that Joe was complaining. It was preferable to whatever had led to Tom's bruised knuckles.

Dropping his pillow and blanket on the armchair to his right, Joe handed over the remaining blanket to Tom, who took it with a "thank you," his gaze going to Joe's armchair.

"You're not planning on sleeping there, are you?" Tom asked.

"How else am I going to keep an eye on you? It's far more comfortable than the floor. Jules said you needed to be observed, so that's what I'm going to do.

I'll wake you up regularly through the night to check you're okay."

"Won't you be uncomfortable?"

"Nah, I'll be fine. I've slept there plenty of times when Bea and the kids have stayed over."

Tom shook his head. "I can't let you do that, Joe. You've done enough for me already. I won't have you sleeping so uncomfortably in your own home because of me."

"You're right," Joe said with a smile and put his hand on Tom's shoulder. "This *is* my home, and I've decided you need to rest and I'm going to keep an eye on you."

"Okay," Tom sighed, giving in. Though Joe could tell he wasn't happy about it.

"It's a bit late for a meal, but how do you feel about some apple and cinnamon pie, and some milk?" Joe asked.

Tom's eyes lit up and he looked about ready to salivate. "That sounds great."

Joe motioned for Tom to follow him and he headed into the kitchen. He tried to tell himself he wasn't nervous about having Tom try his pie. He pointed to the breakfast nook tucked against the corner in his cozy little country-style kitchen and got busy warming up some pie and milk. As he did, he noticed the way Tom took in every inch of the kitchen. Tom did that a lot, it seemed. It was more than curiosity, and a little odd, but he could hardly fault the poor guy for feeling mindful of his surroundings.

Joe's kitchen wasn't the biggest, but it was a decent size, warm and bright with its subdued yellows and reds, the white refrigerator, sink, and appliances all matching. The most expensive and well-used appliance was, of course, his oven.

He walked the pie and milk over to Tom and poured a mugful of juice for himself. "It's not state of the art or anything, but it's got everything I need. My favorite is this nook. There's nothing more relaxing than looking out at the garden in the morning with a fresh cup of coffee, watching the sun shine down on the world." He sat opposite Tom and turned his attention out the window, pretending like he wasn't about to break out into a cold sweat.

Halfway through, Joe noticed Tom's brows had drawn together, and he was staring down at his plate. Maybe this hadn't been such a good idea. Dammit, maybe he should have made the guy some toast. *Get a hold of yourself, Joe. It's just pie.* "Something wrong?"

"No, it's just… it tastes… warm. I mean, not temperature-wise, but like… warmth." Tom looked straight at him, the glow of his smile enough to light up the darkness outside.

"The smell of cinnamon, vanilla… it makes me think of the seaside. Almost like a distant memory, something so far away it's out of reach, but the feeling from it is still very much alive, and so full of love." He looked down at his plate with a frown. "Guess that sounds pretty crazy, huh?" When there was no answer, he looked up at Joe, his eyes going wide. Probably due to the stunned expression on Joe's face. "Joe?"

"My parents used to work a lot when I was a kid," Joe confessed quietly. "They were farmers, born and raised, so they didn't really have many options when they moved to the city. They moved here because they wanted me to have a better life than the one they'd had." Joe shifted awkwardly in his seat and turned his attention back to the window. "On Sundays when they should have been resting, they'd spend every moment of the day with me, taking me all over New York. We'd go to a park or to the beach, Coney Island. We always had picnics with the most amazing pies, cakes, and muffins. The seaside was always my favorite." He met Tom's gaze, and smiled wistfully. "We always had apple and cinnamon pie at the seaside. I wonder what my mother would think of the subtle little changes I made to her recipe." Tom gaped at him, and Joe couldn't help his shy laugh.

"You… *you* made this?" The awe in Tom's voice sent a little shudder through Joe.

"It's just pie," Joe said feeling embarrassed.

"It's not just pie, Joe. I won't let you get away with that. You're sharing a little piece of yourself with the world, and it's… amazing. Something this good that makes you feel something? That's a gift."

For a moment, Joe sat frozen to the spot, trying to figure out if Tom was just being kind, but the very serious expression on Tom's handsome face told him he wasn't. This was ridiculous. No one could *taste* what he had in his heart. Sure, he put everything into his baking, and when he did, he often lost himself in some happy childhood memory, something brief and faint and faraway he would never have or feel again. There was absolutely no possible way Tom—who knew absolutely nothing about Joe, who knew nothing about himself—could have been able to *see* that.

"Joe? What's wrong?"

Joe gave a little start and shook his head. "I'm sorry. It's been a really, *really* long day. We're both tired, and I think I just got a little caught up in some old memories. I'm fine." No one had ever said anything like that to him before. No one he'd ever known understood him when he talked about tasting memories. They all thought it was him just being screwy again. Now that he was faced with someone who understood, he didn't know what to do.

"Are you sure?"

Joe nodded. "I'm going to try and get some sleep. Tomorrow we can do some online searches, see what we can find. You finish up, and I'll leave the lamp on so you won't trip over anything." Tom didn't look convinced, and Joe was grateful when he didn't push him on the matter.

He left the kitchen and made his way to the small but tidy bathroom. After closing the door, he leaned against the sink. Tomorrow, Jules would tell them how to help Tom, Joe would do it, send the man on his way, and his life would go back to the way it had been. Wouldn't it? Yes, it would. It had to. After brushing his teeth, he was ready for some much-needed sleep. Joe quietly made his way back to the living room and turned off the lights, leaving just the warm glow of the lamp on the wood coffee table. Then he fluffed his pillow and snuggled under his blanket in the armchair. He'd drifted off to sleep when he dazedly heard his name being called.

"Joe? Are you asleep?"

Damn. He must have been really tired. The room was dark with only the glow of the moon filtering in through the window. Tom must have turned off the lamp at some point, but instead of sleeping, he sat on the couch, a blanket wrapped around him while he watched Joe. Here Joe was supposed to be keeping an eye on Tom, not the other way around. *Nice job, Joe.* "Not yet."

"I meant what I said earlier. You've got a gift, Joe. You might not see it, but I do."

Not entirely sure what he was meant to say to that, Joe still smiled. "Thanks, Tom. If you need anything, just let me know."

"You're welcome, Joe. I will. Good night."

A few seconds later, Joe fell asleep, a smile still on his face.

Chapter Four

DARKNESS.

He lay in wait in the shadows, silently listening. There was something he had to do, something important. His life was on the line. Why couldn't he remember? A sharp pain exploded in the back of his skull, and he fell to his knees, wheezing, and feeling sick to his stomach. They knew! They had to. A heavy weight barreled on top of him, and he struggled with what strength remained, his blood running cold, knowing they had every intention of killing him. They wanted him dead. Why? His head was fuzzy, and the darkness was growing inside, threatening to take over. He couldn't let them… couldn't….

Someone called out, reached out for him, but he couldn't tell if it was someone else looking to put an end to his life. What was happening? The pain was crippling, and his muscles tensed, his body prepared to defend itself. He wouldn't die, not here, not now, not after everything he'd done. A fierce cry escaped him, and he sprang up, knocking the mass off him and wrestling it to the ground. He pinned strong arms beneath him, surprised when the body stilled, and he heard a soft, lulling voice that had a strange, calming effect on him.

"Tom, it's me, it's Joe. It's okay. No one's going to hurt you. You were having a nightmare. You remember me, right?"

Tom? Was that his name? He blinked down, his eyes meeting wide eyes the color of the ocean. The seaside.... "Joe?"

A shaky smile came onto the man's face. "Yeah, that's right. It's Joe."

Sweet, jittery, bashful Joe, who had taken him in and been so kind to him. Joe, whose handsome face was filled with such tenderness, flooding Tom's entire being with a feeling he couldn't describe but wanted to bask in. It had been so long since anyone looked at him that way. He couldn't remember, but he could *feel* it. He found himself unable to move. Instead, he lowered himself, wrapping his hands around Joe's head as he nuzzled his face in the crook of Joe's neck. Just for a minute. He needed someone to hold on to. Someone he could trust. He didn't know Joe, but for some strange reason, he felt he could trust him. He desperately wanted to.

"What's happening to me, Joe? Why can't I remember?"

Joe wrapped his arms tightly around Tom's back, rubbing comfortingly with strong hands. It had been so long since he'd trusted someone or felt like he wasn't alone. Was he alone? Why did the thought of trusting someone—anyone—leave him feeling cold?

"I don't know what's happening, but we'll figure it out, okay?" Joe's voice was almost a whisper, the sadness and pain subtly woven into his mellow baritone akin to Tom's. For a moment it was almost as if Joe had read his thoughts. What would have happened to him if Joe hadn't found him? Somehow he felt there was more than one answer to that question, none of which resulted in anything good. Was it just gratitude that had Tom feeling attached to Joe?

How could he not remember anything about himself, yet put his trust so completely in this man? He was practical, he knew that. Procedure, discipline, levelheadedness were words that came to mind when he thought of himself. His attraction to Joe might not have been foreign to him, but the depth of feelings swirling about his head was very new. Yet for every sensible rebuttal his head offered, his heart overruled each and every one.

Tom pulled back slightly, looking into Joe's eyes, and he lowered his gaze down to Joe's lips. What did Joe taste like? Sweet like his pies? Warm like his smile? It occurred to Tom that he was somewhat of a sappy romantic, which felt at odds with the source of his current predicament. It was hard to concentrate with Joe under him. Speaking of hard….

Something stirred down south, and Joe's eyes widened, as did Tom's. Tom scrambled up, and quickly deposited himself on the end of the couch, his hands clamped tightly on his lap while Joe sat himself on the other end, looking everywhere but at Tom. He turned on the small lamp, his gaze on the floor.

Good God, what the hell was wrong with him? How could just thinking about a kiss make him hard so quickly? Joe probably thought he was some kind of pervert, wrestling him to the ground and then getting hard like that.

"I'm so sorry. I don't know what came over me. That's never happened before." The man had saved his life, and this was how he showed his gratitude? "At least I don't think so. I, uh, maybe it's been a while for me too." Tom needed to calm down. This really wasn't the time or place. When he glanced at Joe, he noticed how Joe's cheeks were flushed, his legs crossed, and he darted his gaze around the room to avoid Tom. "Would you mind if I use your bathroom?"

"You don't have to ask, Tom. This is your home while you're here," Joe replied somewhat unsteadily. He cleared his throat and motioned to the kitchen. "I'm going to, um, get some water."

Tom nodded and sat there.

Joe didn't budge.

"Should I…? Okay, I'll go first." Tom jumped to his feet and rushed down the hall to the bathroom. He closed the door and went to the sink, where he splashed his face with cold water. What the hell was wrong with him? He wiped the excess water from his face before studying himself in the mirror, willing himself to remember something—*anything*. Closing his eyes, he took a deep breath and tried to recall. It was all in there beyond the veil of blurred shapes and colors. Faceless people, muffled voices. What if his memory didn't come back? He quickly shook himself. Whatever happened, he'd figure it out. He was a survivor. Holding up one of his hands, he flexed his fingers, his bruised and reddened skin stretching over his knuckles. Whoever had hurt him, he'd hurt them back. At least that was something.

With a sigh, he dried his face and turned off the light before heading into the living room. Joe was huddled in the armchair under his blanket. He was pretending to be asleep. Tom had no idea how he knew that, but he did. With a small smile, he went back to the couch. If Joe wanted to pretend whatever had happened hadn't happened, then Tom would go along with it. He owed Joe that much.

Tom woke the next morning to the most amazing smells: the aroma of freshly brewed coffee and the mouthwatering whiff of baked pastries. His stomach growled, demanding to be introduced to the source of such decadence. Getting up, he stretched and noticed his jeans and T-shirt had been cleaned and carefully draped over Joe's armchair, along with his leather jacket. The clock on the mantel said it was nine in the morning. Wow, had he really slept that late? Guessing by his reaction, sleeping in wasn't something he did often, and considering he'd slept on a couch, he was even more surprised by it. How early had Joe gotten up to get Tom's clothes washed *and* bake whatever smelled so good?

He padded down the hall to the bathroom, and after washing up, shaving, and running a comb through his disheveled hair, he got dressed, smiling at the feel of his own clothes—the only thing connecting him to the man he was. They fit perfectly, from his dark jeans and charcoal-gray long-sleeved T-shirt to his black socks and boots. He looked himself over in the mirror. Not much color in his wardrobe, but it felt right. The clothes were good quality, and his jacket a designer brand. Suddenly, a thought struck him. They'd taken his wallet but left a really expensive jacket behind.

With a frown, he looked down at his boots. They were worth a few hundred, easy. Why not take the boots? He couldn't have had much in his wallet. Not more than what the boots and jacket were worth combined. What had he been doing in a garden, anyway? It was a strange place to end up, not to mention get mugged. Maybe he should check his jacket. Joe had mentioned there was no ID or anything on him, but maybe he missed something.

Tom found his jacket and sat down on the couch with it, carefully inspecting every pocket both outside and inside. He patted the sleeves and felt up the lining. He had no idea what he was looking for, but if he could just find *something*, he might have a lead. The motions seemed familiar to him.

With a renewed sense of purpose, he went over his jacket inch by inch, checking every stitch, every inch of fabric. His heart sank when all he found were traces of dirt and pink flower petals inside his right pocket. Dammit. With a heavy sigh, he threw his jacket on the couch cushion beside him. For a moment, he thought he might have found something, no matter how minimal.

Well, he wasn't going to learn anything new moping around on the couch. He stood and walked to the kitchen when he heard the lovely melody of an old jazz song. He laid his head against the chipped wood of the door with a smile, letting the lyrics of some sweet love song wash over him. Just the thought of Joe made his insides go all warm again. Amazing. The man didn't even have to be in the room and he managed to lift Tom's spirit. Why?

This thing he had going on with Joe, it was strange. He shouldn't feel this way about someone he'd known for such a small amount of time. Joe had every right to be cautious. Slowly, he pushed the swinging door open and peeked inside, biting his lip to keep himself from chuckling at the sight of Joe bouncing along to the tapping cymbals and vivacious brass, a tray of muffins in his mitted hands and a blue-and-white-striped apron tied around his waist, the color making his eyes seem more blue than green. Slipping inside, Tom watched Joe for a bit before speaking. "Morning, sunshine."

"Jesus!" Muffins shot off the tray in a desperate attempt to escape, landing on the floor. Joe gazed down at the little scattered breads, lips pursed. "I dropped my muffins."

"Man, I'm so sorry." Tom quickly got to cleaning up the mess. "I'll help you bake some more." He tried not to laugh at the truly leery expression on Joe's face. As if Tom had suggested they secretly use his baked goods as a means to smuggle illegal contraband out of the country.

After a quick shake of his head to snap himself out of it, Joe smacked Tom's hand away. "Stop sneaking up on me like that, and *maybe* I'll let you help. Hopefully, the extent of your culinary prowess is better than Donnie's."

Having collected what was left of the rogue baked goods, Joe stood and Tom followed him over to the large wooden table in the center of the kitchen where Joe replaced his food gloves with new ones.

"I take it the kid's not the greatest cook," Tom said. Not that he was any kind of expert himself. Or was he? Something told him he did okay, but wasn't really any kind of chef. He loved food as much as the next guy, but the thought of sweating away over a hot stove didn't appeal to him.

"Have you ever seen bread spontaneously combust?" Joe asked casually. Tom shook his head. "Well, I have. I tell you, it's heartbreaking. I'm still trying to figure out how he did it."

Tom laughed, leaning his elbows on the table only to get a light smack on the arm.

"I prepare food on here. Go wash up to your elbows. And stop with the face."

Rubbing his arm as if it was sore, Tom's brows rose inquisitively. "What face?"

"*That* face." Joe pushed the tip of his index finger against the end of Tom's nose, his eyes narrowed. "The puppy face."

"I have a puppy face?" Somehow he was pretty sure puppy was not a term often associated with him. Tom tried not to let too much of his amusement show. Joe would probably whack him again. He cleared his throat and nodded very somberly. "I'll uh, keep that in mind."

Deciding it was best to let Joe get on with whatever he was doing, Tom did as Joe asked and washed. When he was done, he pulled a stool over to the end of the table, content to just watch until he was given something specific to do. He noticed the multitude of ingredients scattered about. He would never have guessed it took all that to make a pie. There was flour, brown sugar, lemon juice, a collection of little bottles that appeared to be extracts, smaller containers with powders of which Tom could distinctly smell cinnamon—a scent he was coming to associate with Joe and loving more every minute. There were scores of different sized ceramic bowls and wooden utensils. To one side of Joe was a piecrust he must have made while Tom was asleep, and in front of him a big bowl of red fruitiness.

"What's that?" Tom asked curiously.

"This is the filling for my cherry pie." Joe's smile lit the room, and Tom smiled too. Though lately, he seemed to always find himself smiling. It felt… nice.

"Is that your favorite?"

Joe stared at him. "How'd you know that?"

"You have a big, sappy grin on your face."

"As opposed to the big, sappy one on yours?" Joe snorted, mixing his cherry filling. "I offer three different pies a day. Today is Thursday, so it's cherry, chocolate cream, and blackberry. Fridays is lemon, banana cream, and peanut butter. Saturdays it's caramel with pecan, strawberry, and key lime. Sundays we're closed. Mondays we have pecan, cranberry with apple, and blueberry. Tuesdays it's apple, lemon meringue, and peach. Wednesdays we have apple and cinnamon, coconut cream, and pear. All the pies for today have already been made and are being eaten as we speak. This is for later. As soon as I'm done, we'll go downstairs and have some breakfast."

"Wow." It was all Tom could think of to say. The man was amazing. "How long have you been up?"

"Since four thirty. I slept in a little," Joe replied, his cheeks going a little rosy.

"Jesus, there's a four thirty?" Tom asked, only half joking. "Wait, *that's* sleeping in for you?"

Joe rolled his eyes. "Yes, there is a four thirty. If I woke up at nine every morning, I wouldn't have any customers. It's sleeping in for me Monday through Friday. Saturday we open up later. I'm usually up before five. Sundays I sleep in until seven or eight."

"I don't always sleep in until nine," Tom stated, feeling somewhat affronted. He wasn't quite sure how he knew that, but he was somehow sure. "Unless I'm out really late. I don't really keep regular hours. Besides, it's not as if my routine has been normal lately."

"Tom, not everyone likes mornings. It's nothing to get defensive about," Joe went on, adding a pinch of something to the bowl of cherry filling and looking as calm as could be. Meanwhile, Tom frowned.

"I wouldn't feel defensive even if I didn't like mornings, but as it happens, I do like mornings, very much," Tom huffed, crossing his arms over his chest.

"You seem a little cranky this morning. Why don't you go back to sleep for a while. Maybe you'll feel better when you wake up."

"I'm not cranky! I don't want to go back to sleep." He pouted. Why was he pouting? Joe was right—he was being cranky. Dammit.

Joe gave him a pointed look. "There's that face again."

"What face!" After an exasperated sigh, Tom decided it best he take a deep breath and assess the situation. Somewhere, something went awry, and after backtracking a moment, he realized that something was him. "Okay, maybe I am a little cranky this morning. I'm sorry." What the hell had gotten into him? He wasn't normally prone to angry outbursts. Was he? No, he was sure he wasn't. Aw, hell, he didn't even know which way he was facing anymore, and that wasn't good for either of them.

"What's wrong?" Joe cleaned his hands on a paper towel and turned to him, all patience and understanding, making Tom feel like a jerk.

"It's just so damn irritating," he said. "Every time I feel I might be on the verge of remembering something, that cloud—that fuzzy image of colors, shapes, and sounds pulsing in my mind's eye—just stops and stays there, floating and taunting me. Like a melody you can hear clearly in your head but can't quite remember the lyrics or the voice that goes with it. I thought I'd find something in my jacket that would put me on the right track to remembering who I am. Maybe something we missed in the lining." He shook his head. "Nothing but dirt."

"Yeah, you were kind of covered in the stuff. It was in your pockets too. Thought I'd gotten all of it. I'm sorry, Tom. We'll find a lead. You'll see. Getting yourself worked up and frustrated isn't going to do you any good, all right? Some hot breakfast, good coffee, and you'll be all set for sleuthing. I'll see to it that Bea whips up something special for us. Then we can come back up here, grab my laptop, and see what we can find."

How did the man do that? A few words and Tom felt like he could take on the world. If Joe told him it would be okay, Tom had no doubts that it would be. He found himself feeling lighthearted again.

"Thanks, Joe."

"No problem," Joe replied with a sweet smile that made Tom's pulse quicken. Then he realized what Joe said.

"Us? You mean you haven't had breakfast yet?"

Joe's cheeks flushed while he went back to his ingredients. "No, I thought it'd be best if we had breakfast together. You know, to make it easier for Bea," he explained feebly, not tearing his gaze away from the table. "Less for her to worry about."

Joe waiting to eat breakfast had nothing to do with convenience. Tom held back a smile. "Thanks."

Joe nodded, going back to his baking, and Tom went back to watching him, mesmerized by Joe's graceful hands as he stirred the mixture, adding dashes and drops of various ingredients, a faraway look coming onto his handsome face, one he seemed to get when involved with his pies.

Despite the daydreaming, Joe's hands never missed a beat, and he scooped the filling into the piecrust. Once it was all in, he removed his gloves and swiped his finger along the inside of the bowl. Tom nearly fell off his chair when Joe sucked and licked his finger, completely oblivious to how incredibly arousing the gesture was. *Down, boy.*

After scooping up some more filling, Joe started to move his finger to his mouth when Tom caught his wrist, snapping him out of his little trance. Looking from his finger to Tom, Joe cocked his head to one side in question. Tom didn't say a word. He let every bit of his hunger show in his eyes as he very deliberately drew Joe's finger into his mouth, provoking the gorgeous man to draw a sharp breath. The ocean of his blue-green eyes grew stormy while he stood transfixed by Tom's tongue as it ran over the gooey, red digit. A tremor went through Joe, and Tom grinned wickedly.

"Mm, do you always taste so fruity?"

Joe arched an eyebrow. "Is that a bad pun? Because if it is, you're cute, but you're not *that* cute."

Tom laughed. He had an overwhelming urge to kiss Joe, but that would be a bad idea. Reining in his wayward thoughts, he averted his gaze. "Thanks for washing my clothes."

Joe fidgeted with his apron before turning back to his ingredients. "No problem."

"JOE? Where are you?"

"Oh!" Joe smiled brightly and turned toward the door. "We're in here, Jules."

Tom watched curiously as the kitchen door opened and a petite, young woman with soft red curls stepped in. When she saw Joe, she dropped her backpack on the floor and flung herself into his arms.

"It's so good to see you!"

Jules was pretty, dressed in jeans and a deep green band T-shirt that brought out her big emerald eyes. Her fiery hair and her crimson lipstick sharp against her pale skin, and she was curvy in all the right places. When she saw Tom observing her, she pulled away from Joe and extended a hand to him. "You must be Joe's new friend."

"Tom. Well, that's the name we're going with for the time being."

"It's a pleasure, Tom. Don't you worry. You're in very good hands," she said confidently, motioning to Joe. "And don't you let him tell you otherwise."

"Right, well, Tom," Joe cut in before Jules could say any more. It was apparent the little redhead knew her friend quite well. "Jules is a great nurse—better than some of the doctors she works with." He crossed his arms over his chest and frowned. "That jackass still giving you trouble? Because I'll go down there and give him a piece of my mind."

Jules laughed and patted Joe's arm soothingly. "I know you would, Joe. No need. That jackass won't be bothering me anymore."

Tom straightened at the sad smile that came onto her face, just as Joe's arms fell at his sides.

"What happened?" Joe asked.

"They laid me off this morning," she sighed.

"What!" Joe took hold of her shoulders. "I don't understand. Why? How? You're the best nurse they have!"

"Come on, Joe. Times are tough, you know that. Budget cuts. I was lucky they didn't let me go sooner, what with my being the only one in that clinic with a set of ovaries." Her eyes teared up, but with a deep breath, she blinked them back and straightened, giving Joe a hearty pat on the shoulder. "Don't worry. I already have two interviews lined up for next week. So really, I'll be just fine. Now, Tom." She turned to Tom with a cheerful smile and motioned to the door. "Why don't we go into the living room so you can be more comfortable, and we'll see what we can do?"

"Okay." He followed Jules out, Joe trailing behind, and sat on the edge of the couch while she pulled a stethoscope out of her bag.

She smiled warmly. "Okay, Tom. I'll need you to take off your shirt."

"Sure." He did his best not to notice Joe's sudden fixation with the lampshade on the small wooden table. After removing his shirt, Tom laid it on the couch beside him as Jules placed the stethoscope to his chest over his heart. He took the opportunity to sneak a peek over at Joe, who was very blatantly staring at his chest. A little shiver went through Tom, and he had to remember he was in the middle of an examination.

Jules smiled widely. "Sorry, the diaphragm's always cold at first."

"Oh, right, of course." Tom cleared his throat, and Jules glanced at Joe, who was studying the lampshade with great interest and an even greater blush on his cheeks. She turned her attention back to Tom and gave him a conspiratorial wink.

"Okay, Tom. Deep breath, and release slowly. Good. Again."

He did as asked, conscious of Joe's gaze on him every time he breathed deeply. Patiently, he sat as Jules took his blood pressure, checked his pupils, felt the now significantly reduced bump on his head, and continued her thorough examination of him. She had very warm and gentle hands, and he immediately felt at ease with her. Once she was done, she started asking him a series of simple questions. He could do math just fine, and he remembered TV shows and movies. He knew the sky was for the most part blue, depending on what state you were in. That you used a spoon to eat soup and who the president was, among various other odd facts.

"Do you remember everything that's happened after your injury?"

"Anything that's happened since waking up on Joe's couch I remember just fine. Before that, I get hints of memories, fuzziness. Figures but no faces, more like shadows. I can't recall any names or feel any familiarity."

"What's the verdict?" Joe asked, his tone filled with concern.

"You're in great shape, Tom, apart from the memory loss. Obviously anything more in-depth would require the proper analysis and tests." She put away her equipment as she spoke, her voice calm and soothing. "I'm afraid without hospitalization, it's hard to know for sure, but from what I can gather, it's only temporary. Tom, you'll recover, and I'm certain your brain is starting the process as we speak, but it could take some time. Your semantic memory is fine. That's the conscious recollection of your general knowledge. Whatever you knew how to do before, like drive, read, scramble eggs, hasn't been affected." She placed her hand on Tom's shoulder and gave it a reassuring squeeze.

"I know it's frustrating, but you were very lucky. Whoever did that to you could have killed you, or if they'd hit you in the right place, just hard enough, your injuries could have been so much worse. Some patients lose the ability to form any new memories. Yours will come back. There's no telling how it'll come back, however. With this sort of thing, it's not just a matter of someone just telling you who you are. That won't necessarily bring everything back, nor will just looking at something. Listen to your body when it talks to you, your instincts, feelings you get about certain things, smells and sounds. If you need anything, or just need to talk, you call me, okay? Joe's got my number."

"Thank you, Jules, I really do appreciate it," Tom replied, sitting back glumly. He didn't know what he'd expected. It wasn't as if she had some magic pill that would undo everything.

Joe took a seat beside him and placed a hand on his shoulder. "It'll be okay, Tom. You'll see."

Tom nodded and gave him a small smile, glad he wasn't alone.

"Joe?" Jules interrupted quietly. "Would you mind escorting me downstairs? I'd like to say hi to Bea and the kids before going."

Joe looked a little uncertain about leaving him, so Tom smiled broadly, not wanting to be any more of an inconvenience to Joe. He didn't want to take over the man's life. After all, Joe had friends, and a business to run. "You go ahead, Joe. I'll be fine."

"Okay," Joe nodded. "I'll be back in a minute."

Joe and Jules left, and Tom sat there in silence for a moment, looking around the cozy apartment. One wall was exposed brick, the rest painted a nice cream color. The furniture was slightly worn but comfortable, the sofa and armchair a pleasant chocolate color with quilted throw pillows. A plush clean rug lay on the wood floor, and the rest of the furniture was dark oak, from the bookshelves flanking the small entertainment center to the coffee table. Vintage prints of coffee and old New York City were elegantly framed and painstakingly arranged along the walls. There wasn't much by the way of trinkets, but the mantel above the small fireplace had photos. It wasn't fancy, by any means, but it was clean, tidy, and comfortable.

Tom was used to bigger surroundings. For some reason that occurred to him just then. Something about Joe's place felt so warm… like his life had been lacking in it for a long time. Did he want to remember who he was? Of course he did. How could he not? He wanted to know where he came from, what he did for a living, his own damned name, for Christ's sake. Mostly he wanted to know the kind of man he was. He couldn't lose faith. After all, he had Joe. And for now, that was more than enough.

Chapter Five

THIS should be interesting.

Jules had that look on her face. One Joe knew too well. He escorted her down the steps leading into the hallway just outside the shop's kitchen, bracing himself when she came to a stop at the bottom. Something was weighing on her mind, something she didn't want to say in front of Tom.

Jules turned to him, her lovely face filled with genuine affection. He'd known Jules since she was in college, coming into the shop for her mandatory cup of coffee in the morning, chatting away to Joe about everything and anything. They'd gotten along from the first day, when she'd asked Joe to marry her after taking a bite of his pie.

"I'm sorry about your job, sweetheart."

"It's okay, Joe," Jules said with a smile and a shrug. "I have no intention of giving up so easily. If it's worth having, it's worth fighting for, right? Joe, Tom should really go to a hospital. He needs proper medical attention."

With a deep frown, Joe shook his head. "I've tried. There's no talking him into it. I promised to help him, and I have every intention of doing that. Is that what's on your mind?" He peered at her warily. "Because I know that look."

Mischief twinkled in her big green eyes. "You like him."

"What?" Where had *that* come from?

"Don't even try it. I saw the way you two were eye-sexing each other."

Joe gasped. "I was not eye-sexing him!"

"You so were. And you wouldn't stop blushing! There you go, blushing again!"

Dammit! Was he that obvious? He dared to sneak a peek at her and groaned at the smug smile on her face. Nothing got past Jules. She had a way of making him squirm under that sharp gaze of hers. It was like she took lessons from Bea or something.

"He *is* hot," Jules added with a wicked smile.

Joe's eyes widened as he clamped a hand over her mouth. "You're not supposed to notice things like that," he whispered hoarsely. "You're a nurse."

"With eyes," Jules muttered after moving his hand away from her mouth. "Tom is not my patient. He's a friend of yours who I was helping out. Joe, don't you go shying away from this one. Not only is he gorgeous, but he's clearly attracted to you. He kept sneaking glances at you the entire time I was examining him. I thought my stethoscope was going to melt from the heat he was giving off."

"Why is everyone so concerned about my love life?" he grumbled.

"Probably because you haven't had one in over a decade." Her expression softened. "You two need each other, Joe. You deserve someone who will treat you right and make you happy."

"The man doesn't remember who he is, Jules. What if he has someone?" Even if Tom didn't, it wasn't the 'falling for someone' part that had Joe worried. It was everything else that went with it, and everything that came after. That was the average relationship. What he had with Tom, he couldn't even begin to comprehend. There were more unknowns in this mess than there were holes in Swiss cheese. "Besides, I don't want Tom to be with me because he feels indebted to me." He didn't know whether he was saying that for Jules's benefit, or his own.

Jules gave his arm a sympathetic pat. "Give the man more credit than that. You think a man like that's going to hang around someone just because he feels he owes something? Being grateful is one thing. Wanting to jump a guy's bones is something else."

"For crying out loud," Joe groaned. "You've been gossiping with Bea again, haven't you?"

Jules let out a giggle. "No more than the usual. I'm just saying, don't get so caught up in what you don't know and pay attention to what you do know. Take a chance. The man lost his memory, but who he is at his core hasn't changed."

Joe could stand here all day, giving perfectly logical reasons as to why he shouldn't jump headfirst into this insanity, and get no closer to changing Jules's already made-up mind than he was now, so he gave up.

If only he had half the doggedness the women in his life possessed.

Letting out a little sigh, Jules shook her head. "Joe, I hate to say it but, you *knew* the kind of man Blake was, and look what happened there."

Again with Blake. The man seemed to torture him even years after Joe had the misfortune of getting involved with him. Every time he thought about it, he felt like such an idiot, even more of an idiot than Blake had made him feel at the time. "Exactly how is that an argument *against* what I'm saying?"

"I'm saying it because you can't have one rotten jerk ruin your chances at happiness. You deserve better, Joe." She stood on her toes and kissed his cheek. "Look after him. Tom's going to be feeling frustrated and miserable. You'll want to reassure him, get his mind off trying to force things. All it's going to do is give him a headache."

"I will." He gave her a kiss in return and squeezed her tight. "You take care, sweetheart, and call me if you need anything at all."

"You bet." With a wink she was gone, and Joe released a steady breath. He sure hoped she was right. Well, he'd promised Tom they'd do some online sleuthing, so he best get to it. He asked Bea to make him and Tom a hearty breakfast before he ran upstairs. Inside his apartment, Tom stood by the window, looking out. He looked so lost. Joe had gotten used to Tom's big dopey grin, and seeing him without one was just… wrong. Maybe he couldn't do much in the way of helping Tom remember, but he could damn well help him keep his spirits up.

"Hey, Tom. Hope you're hungry. Bea's making us enough food to feed an army."

Tom gave a little start and turned. His smile nearly took Joe's breath away. "Hey, you came back."

"Of course I came back. What? Did you think I was going to forget my promise to feed you?" Joe teased.

"I wasn't worried," Tom replied

"I'm just going to get my laptop. Be right back." Joe hurried to his bedroom and grabbed the laptop from his small desk in the corner. He brought it out and motioned to the couch. Taking a seat, he hadn't expected Tom to sit so close. Their legs were all but pressed up against each other. Of course when he opened his laptop, he realized Tom's proximity was likely due to him wanting to see the screen rather than any desire to plaster himself to Joe.

Trying his best not to fidget, Joe booted up the laptop then opened his browser. "Why don't we start with missing persons?" Tom gave him a nod and Joe looked up the NYPD Missing Person's database. They started with Manhattan, scanning all the photos. When they found no matches, they moved onto the other boroughs. Tom was tense beside Joe, and the closer they got to the end of the final borough's listing, the more Tom fidgeted.

"Nothing." Tom sighed. He glanced over at Joe, his expression unreadable. "I guess that leaves the Wanted list."

Joe couldn't bring himself to say anything. He gave Tom a curt nod and clicked on the Wanted link in the sidebar. What if Tom was on that list? Tom pushed to his feet and started pacing.

This was a bad idea. If Tom *was* on there, at least they'd have more information, but it would also mean it was Joe's moral obligation to inform the police. Seeming to sense his hesitation, Tom turned to face him.

"Do it, Joe. I have to know. Whatever comes up… we'll deal with it then."

Joe nodded. He stopped overthinking, and started going through the extensive list of victims and perpetrators. Once he'd scrolled through the list, he played all the Crime Stoppers videos. A huge sense of relief washed over him. "Nothing."

Tom visibly relaxed. "Okay. That's good, right? I mean, at least I'm not wanted in New York City."

Which of course didn't mean he wasn't wanted elsewhere. As if reading his thoughts, Tom resumed his seat on the couch beside Joe. "Maybe we should have a look at the surrounding states?"

For the next couple of hours, they searched the Missing Persons databases for the surrounding states, along with their Wanted listings, and got nothing each time. Bea had brought them their breakfast, and they'd eaten on the floor picnic-style while Joe continued to search. There was no sign of Tom on the web. Giving up that search, Joe pulled up a website on baby names and went through the list with Tom to see if any of them might jog his memory.

Nothing.

Moving on, they tried scrolling through the different state websites, looking up pictures, monuments, towns, but nothing triggered anything in Tom's memory.

"I think we've done enough for one day," Joe suggested softly. He could see Tom growing more despondent with every nothing they turned up. He shut his laptop and tossed it onto the couch cushion beside him.

"Joe, we need to talk about how I'm going to earn my keep."

"What are you talking about?"

"I can't just live off your generosity. It could be weeks, even months before I might remember anything. I'm grateful to you for letting me stay, but you have to let me do something. I can help you downstairs taking out the trash, washing dishes, serving. You name it and I'll do it. Please, Joe. It's the only way I'll feel good about you putting yourself out for my sake." Tom looked around the room and sighed. "Also, I need to keep busy or I'll go crazy. I'm not very good with sitting still for very long, or being cooped up."

Joe wanted to protest that having Tom's company was hardly putting Joe out, but Tom was right. Keeping him busy would be a good idea. He seemed like the type of guy who wouldn't be content sitting around doing nothing. "All right, since it's so important to you. You can help me in the kitchen downstairs. Believe me, you'll be plenty busy, but it'll keep you from being spotted. The garden between the shop and the boutique next door is locked and shrouded enough where you can go out if you need some air but can keep out of sight. How's that?"

"That's great! Thank you." He gave Joe a hearty squeeze.

"Okay, okay," Joe replied with a gentle shove. "You're really touchy-feely, aren't you?"

Tom grinned sheepishly. "Sorry, can't seem to help myself around you."

"Well, please do." At Tom's faltering smile, Joe cleared his throat. "At least in the shop, you know. The last thing we need is Bea trying to get us to pick out color swatches or china together."

"Right." Tom chuckled. "She's pretty persuasive."

"She also raised five mountainesque boys, one of whom went on to play professional football, so the woman's got whacking skills. Do exactly what she says and you won't end up with her handprint on your ass."

Tom stared at him. "I'll, uh, keep that in mind."

"Good. Let's get baking."

JOE had to admit he'd been a little apprehensive about having Tom downstairs in the shop, even if it was just in the kitchen. He'd been worried Tom would get bored or frustrated. Tom surprised them all. He was quick to adapt, and after having something explained to him once, he picked up a knack as if he'd always been doing it. By midweek, Tom knew his way around the kitchen like he'd been working there all his life. Despite being unable to recall past memories, his mind was sharp. Bea was left speechless, and Joe had even taken a picture on his cell phone for posterity, and proof the impossible had been achieved.

"That boy is something else," Bea murmured at Joe behind the counter up front. "He's memorized all the ingredients for all our pies and exactly how much of what goes in which. And he's darn quick. You should see the way he handles a knife. I've never seen anything like it. I wish I could say he might be a chef, but"—Bea looked up at Joe, her concern evident—"not with the way he moves. Very precise. Methodical. Procedural. The way he remembers every detail? The boy's had some kind of training."

Joe swallowed hard and did his best to smile. "I think you're overthinking this, Bea." A thought occurred to Joe. "Do you think he might be in the military?" Why hadn't he thought of that before? "It makes sense. He's in really good shape."

Bea considered that. She was about to reply when the little bell above the door rang. Joe turned to greet his new customers with a smile, but the moment he saw the two men dressed in slacks and leather jackets, the smile fell off his face. Something about them gave Joe pause. One of them smiled politely as they approached the counter.

"Mr. Applin?"

"Yes? How can I help you, gentlemen?"

"Could we step outside for a moment?" The taller of the two men looked around the shop before returning his smile to Joe. He leaned in to speak quietly. "We don't want to alarm your customers."

"Um, sure." Joe gave Bea's arm a reassuring squeeze and followed the men out the front door onto the busy sidewalk. They stepped to one side, away from the shop window, and showed Joe their badges.

"Mr. Applin, I'm Detective Romero, and this is my partner, Detective McCrea, NYPD. We're looking for a man we believe is in the area. He's about six foot four, two hundred and ten pounds, black hair, gray eyes, and was last seen wearing dark jeans, black shirt, boots, and a leather jacket. Have you seen him?"

"A lot of folks come into my shop," Joe replied, pretending to give the question real thought. What should he do? Maybe these men could help Tom. Or maybe they were here to arrest him. "Is this man in some kind of trouble?"

"I'm afraid we can't disclose any information at this time, but he's wanted for questioning. We just want to talk to him."

Joe opened his mouth, but instead of the truth, he went with his gut. "I'm afraid I haven't seen him. I would have remembered someone like that." He gave them an apologetic smile. "I'm sorry I couldn't be more help, but if I see him I'll certainly let you know. Do you have a card or number where I could reach you?"

The taller man smiled again. "No problem, Mr. Applin. We'll be in touch. Thank you for your time."

With a nod, the two walked off, murmuring to each other quietly. Something wasn't sitting right with Joe. He casually went back inside and to the counter, where he finished ringing up a customer.

"Who were they?" Bea asked. "Looked like thugs to me."

"They were asking for Tom," Joe replied quietly as he removed his apron. "Would you and the kids close up for me, Bea? I need to have a word with Tom."

"What did you tell them?"

"That I hadn't seen him. I don't trust those men."

"Joe…."

It wasn't like Bea to look so worried. He'd brought her enough worry over the years. He gave her cheek a kiss. "Don't you worry, Bea. I'll take care of it. It'll be fine."

Bea didn't look happy about it, but she nodded and went back to work. Joe went into the kitchen where he found Tom and Donnie huddled together, smiling like a couple of kids.

"What are you two up to?"

Donnie glanced up with a huge grin. "Tom's showing me how to do something."

"Oh?"

Tom turned to Joe and held out his hand. "For you."

Joe blinked down at the apple in Tom's hand. Except it wasn't just an apple. It had been carved into a rose.

"I don't know what to say." Joe took the apple and inspected it. Each petal had been sliced to perfection.

"It's… beautiful." He felt like a bit of a jerk now. Tom looked happy and Joe was about to take that smile away. He had no choice. He had to let Tom know. "Thanks, Tom." Joe couldn't help the way his stomach filled with butterflies when Tom winked. "Could we go upstairs? I need to talk to you about something."

"Sure." Tom gave Donnie a gentle pat on the back. "Keep practicing. Elsie will love it."

"Thanks, Tom." Donnie beamed at him and went back to carving his apple.

Tom followed Joe upstairs to the apartment and into the kitchen. It was Joe's favorite room and made him feel relaxed. He placed the apple in the center of his table and took a seat at the breakfast nook. Tom followed suit.

"Donnie's a great kid. He's crazy about Elsie. I told him he needs to take a shot at it or he'll never know what could be." Tom cocked his head to one side, his smile fading. "Everything okay, Joe?"

"Yeah, um, I don't know. Two men came into the shop looking for you."

Tom leaned in, his hands gripping the edge of the table. "What? Who?"

"They said they were detectives, showed me their badges. They described you, said you might be in the area, and asked if I'd seen you?"

Tom sat up. "What did you say?"

"That a lot of folks come into my shop. I asked if the man they were looking for was in trouble, and they said they couldn't disclose that information. When I asked if they had a card or a number where I could contact them, they said it wasn't a problem and they'd be in touch."

"Did you ask them anything else?"

Joe frowned. "What else was I supposed to ask them?"

"Jesus, Joe. Anything. Something that might have helped me remember *something*." Tom got to his feet and started pacing. "You could have asked them if they had a name. I could have had a name."

"Oh." The thought hadn't occurred to Joe. "They seemed reluctant to give me any information about you other than your physical description. There's a chance they might not have told me."

"But you don't know that! Dammit, Joe. You could have pressed them for more information. They must know who I am." Tom paced, growing more frustrated by the moment.

Joe had messed up. He should have asked the men for Tom's name. "I'm sorry. Something about them didn't sit right with me. I was… trying to protect you. It was stupid." This could have been their opportunity to find out about Tom, who he was. Those men clearly knew something. Joe felt terrible. He pulled out his cell phone and browsed the web. "I'll find them. They gave me their names. I'll call them and make something up, pretend I saw you and—"

Tom put his hand on Joe's and crouched down beside him, his silver eyes filled with remorse. "I'm sorry, Joe. Here you are doing so much for me, and I snap at you. Please forgive me."

"No, you're right. We had a chance to find out something about you, and I blew it." Joe gently pushed Tom away and stood. "I just—excuse me." He felt like an idiot. He really had been trying to protect Tom. Even if those men were honest detectives looking to help, Joe didn't trust them. Not that he was the greatest judge of character, but there had been something about them. With a sigh he headed into the living room, intent on locking himself away in his bedroom for a while and calling every precinct until he found those detectives and did something useful for a change.

"Joe, wait." Tom caught up to him, taking hold of his arm and turning him. "You didn't blow it. Your gut told you not to trust these guys, and you followed your instinct. You were protecting me, and I appreciate that. This whole thing has me on edge. I didn't mean to take it out on you. I'd never want you to place yourself in a situation you're not comfortable with for my sake." He put his hand to Joe's cheek and Joe leaned into the touch. "Please, forgive me for being such a jackass."

Joe smiled, his face growing warm at Tom's proximity. His words got caught in his throat and all he could do was nod. He was captivated by Tom's smile, by those intense eyes.

And then Tom kissed him.

TOM was lost in Joe's lips. They were soft and sweeter than any pie Tom was sure the man had ever baked. A low, deep moan escaped Joe, sending Tom's senses into turmoil. Joe hesitantly wrapped his strong arms around Tom, and it made Tom's heart thunder in his ears. Joe might be shy, but a fire raged inside him yearning to be stoked, and that only intensified Tom's desire. He gently pushed Joe, forcing him to move back until the back of his legs hit the sofa and he dropped down onto the cushions. Tom didn't falter. He straddled Joe and gave his jaw a small, but firm squeeze.

Tom pushed his tongue against those soft lips, demanding entrance to the heavenly heat that waited inside Joe's mouth. After a brief hesitation on Joe's part, his lips parted and Tom slipped his tongue inside, a thrilling sense of triumph surging through him when Joe moaned. Tom ground his hips down against Joe's so he could feel what he did to Tom, but Joe was still holding back, his spine rigid and his muscles taut.

Reluctantly, Tom tore his mouth away, but only to take Joe's earlobe between his teeth, gently nipping and licking. "Let go, Joe. Just let go. I know this all seems kind of crazy, but I've never felt anything remotely like this for anyone before. I know it. In my heart, I know. There's something about you, and I want to find out what it is. Please let me in."

Something in Joe seemed to snap, and all at once he was scrambling to get Tom's shirt off, pulling it over his head and then tossing it to the floor. He looked Tom over, the lust in his eyes threatening to set Tom ablaze.

"My God, look at you." Joe ran his hands appreciatively over Tom's torso, from the tight muscles of his abdomen up over his chest to his broad shoulders, leaving Tom trembling. He couldn't imagine ever wanting anything as badly as he wanted Joe right this moment, and his need was making him desperate to do some touching of his own. He made quick work of relieving Joe of his apron then T-shirt. Tom thought his heart was going to burst when Joe shyly averted his gaze and wrapped an arm around his torso.

"I'm a baker. Bread and pies are kind of my weakness. I stay in shape, but…." He poked his barely there belly and let out a bashful chuckle. Tom gently took Joe's prodding finger and brought that hand to his lips for a kiss.

He couldn't admire Joe for long without the man getting restless or embarrassed, but he wished Joe knew how beautiful he was. The man was in great shape, sinewy and well-toned, with skin that was amazingly soft. He wasn't all hard muscle like Tom, and somehow that made Joe even more irresistible to him. Tom couldn't explain the feeling, had no idea why certain things came to mind, but touching Joe was… real, honest, and oddly made him feel safe and at home.

"Joe, look at me."

Joe did, hesitantly, his blue-green eyes searching Tom's for… what? Hope? If that was the case, Tom would do everything in his power not to let Joe down. He made no effort to hide the desire he was feeling and he explored Joe's skin as he spoke, his gaze never leaving Joe's. "You're stunning. Every inch of you. I love the way you feel. There's *nothing* I would change, Joe. Nothing." He placed a hand to Joe's chest over his heart, his thumb finding a pink nipple that pebbled under his touch and brought the most delicious whimper from Joe. Tom flicked the little nub, reveling in Joe's gasp as he writhed and wriggled under Tom.

Joe thrust his hips upward as he drew Tom down against him. Good God, he could feel how hard Joe was. All that lay between them was a couple of thin layers of clothing, and it was enough to ignite the fire kindling inside Tom. He picked up his pace, eagerly seeking, *needing* more.

"Tell me what you want, Joe. Anything and it's yours," Tom promised breathlessly, surprised at the realization he meant every word. Something deep down wanted to give Joe everything, wanted to hold him in his arms, protect him from the world, keep him safe and never let go. Despite his lack of memories, something in Tom knew Joe needed that more than he did, needed to be assured he was worthy of unfathomable affection, and damn if Tom didn't want to be the one to do it. Tom trusted his gut. It was something he'd always relied on. Joe was special.

"Kiss me," Joe rasped, almost too low for Tom to hear. "Please."

Those few little words were all Tom needed. Everything inside him sizzled and sparked with life. He captured Joe's mouth and kissed him feverishly, desperate to explore and taste. His body felt like it wanted to consume Joe. Nothing had the power to control the blaze roaring within him except for the timid, beautiful man underneath him.

Tom reached between them and freed their erections, pulling away only long enough to spit into his hand before crushing his mouth back against Joe's and taking them both in hand. Joe's little gasps and moans urged him forward.

"Oh, sweet Jesus," Joe hissed, letting out a shaky breath.

"Is this okay?" Tom breathed, brushing his lips over Joe's cheek. "It feels so damn good, Joe, but I'll stop if you want me to."

"No, don't," Joe all but begged. "Don't stop, Tom. Oh, God…."

Feeling an overwhelming need to please Joe, Tom tightened his grip and quickened his pumping fist, delighting in Joe's sweet sounds as he threw his head back, exposing the smooth, expansive flesh of his neck. Tom took advantage and poked his tongue out to taste and lick Joe from his collarbone to his jaw line.

"You taste like your pies, Joe. So sweet, warm, and full of life."

Joe sprung forward as if some magic switch had been hit, and Tom couldn't help his surprised gasp. His heavy breaths became pants as Joe buried his head against Tom's neck and his hand joined in on the stroking, their hips thrusting wildly and erratically. Joe's grip on Tom was almost painful, and his low growl reverberated against Tom's scorching skin. Cupping his free hand at the back of Joe's neck, Tom held Joe to him as he met every fraught thrust of Joe's hips with one of his own.

"Tom, I—I'm going to—" Joe's words cut off sharply as he cried out, clutching Tom so tightly he was sure there would be some bruising the next day. Joe's body trembled and shook beneath him as he rode his climax, the feel of his warm come coating both their bellies enough for Tom to find his own release. He muffled his hoarse cry against Joe's hair, the silkiness and scent of it swirling around in his head helping him lose himself in the rolling waves of pleasure, their hands milking every last drop from each other.

They slumped together, spent, each man's weight holding up the other, their breathing slowly coming down from the clouds. Joe's chest rose and fell steadily against his own, and Tom could feel himself starting to drift off. He moved his hand and Joe groaned, rousing Tom and reminding him that if he didn't clean them up, they'd get stuck like this.

With his free hand, Tom carefully pushed Joe back into the cushions and leaned forward to place a tender kiss against Joe's lips, smiling when he found the man's eyes closed and his expression one of contentment. His heart swelled, knowing he'd been the one to put it there.

He pulled Joe in for a kiss, the touch of those soft lips a delicious sensation. He willed himself to go slow, allowing his hands to roam over Joe's body, over his arms, his chest, coaxing him to open up. His efforts were rewarded more quickly than he expected, and Joe parted his lips. Not wanting to spook him, he took

Joe's mouth tenderly, his kisses more like caresses. He desperately wanted to feel all of Joe, to touch, taste, and explore every curve, every muscle. It took a great deal of self-control not to let his imagination run away with him. He wrapped his arms around Joe and his sinewy body that fit against Tom's like it was molded to do so.

"You're holding back," Joe murmured against Tom's lips.

"I don't want to rush you."

Joe pulled back, the fire smoldering in those ocean-colored eyes making Tom grateful that he was sitting, because his knees had turned to jelly.

"Why me?" Joe asked quietly, slipping his fingers into Tom's hair and absently stroking. He must have made some kind of noise because Joe chuckled softly. "You like that, huh?"

Tom moaned and let his eyes drift closed. "Oh, yeah. Feels good."

"You didn't answer my question." Joe continued to stroke, and Tom had to be careful he didn't fall asleep right here on Joe's lap. Those long, slender fingers felt so soothing.

"Why *not* you?" Tom smiled when Joe gave his hair a playful tug.

"Look at you. Whoever you are, whatever you do, I'll bet it suits you. I know you're grateful for my help, and I'll still help you, you don't need to—"

"Wait a moment," Tom cut him off, unable to believe what he was hearing. He would have been angry were it not for the utterly wretched look on Joe's handsome face. It made him wonder what could possibly have happened to this sweet man to make him think so little of himself. He remembered Joe saying he'd been hurt, and he couldn't even bear to think of some bastard breaking Joe's heart. A dark, deep-rooted anger bubbled up inside Tom, scaring the hell out of him. He didn't know why he felt so sick to his stomach, but he did his best to push it aside. He took Joe's hands in his and met Joe's reserved gaze.

"Joe, I'm not attracted to you because you're helping me. I can make sense of my own feelings enough to know where they're coming from, and I'm attracted to you because you're beautiful. I'm fascinated by you because you're like no one I've ever met, and I know that because there can't possibly be another man like you out there. I'm sure of it. If I run into a cop, he's probably going to throw me in jail thinking I'm all doped up because I can't keep from grinning like an idiot, and it's all because of you." He ran his thumb over Joe's bottom lip.

"This is crazy. What if you're…? I mean…." Joe had trouble meeting Tom's eyes.

"A criminal? A murderer? A blackmailer?" Tom held back a smile. "A nutritionist?"

Joe jerked away from him, horrified. "Get out."

"Because I might be a murderer or a nutritionist?" Tom teased.

With hands on his hips, Joe narrowed his eyes, a very somber expression on his face. "If you start telling me how much sugar to put into my pies, you're out on your butt. Don't care how cute it is."

"Come here," Tom chuckled, snatching hold of Joe's chin and giving his lips another sweet kiss. "Well, my fillings suggest I'm either not a nutritionist or a real lousy one. Don't you worry. I'm pretty sure I'm none of those things, and if I were…." He sat back, his expression grave. "I'll give it all up for you. Whatever man I may have been in the past, if it makes me someone you'd be disappointed in, I'll stop."

Joe quickly tucked himself away and sat with his bottom lip between his teeth. Tom sorted himself out before getting to his feet. "Hold that thought." He quickly went to the bathroom and washed his hands before grabbing a hand towel and running it under the tap. He returned and handed it to Joe, whose cheeks were flushed as he wiped his hands then his stomach. He folded up the small towel and put it to one side before taking his T-shirt and slipping into it. Tom sat beside him, watching him carefully.

"Joe?" Tom got a queasy feeling in his belly and prayed that he hadn't messed things up. Was Joe regretting what happened? Was he going to ask Tom to leave?

Joe covered his face with his hands. That couldn't be good. When Joe sprang up from the couch so quickly he almost scared the life out of Tom, he started to think the worst. Then again, this was probably normal for Joe. Not what happened on the couch—that was very obviously not normal for Joe—but Joe's restlessness.

"Jesus, what have I done?" Joe paced from one end of the living room to the other so quickly and repeatedly, Tom thought the guy was going to burn a hole in the floor. Figuring he'd better do something before Joe hurt himself, Tom got to his feet and tried to stop Joe, but the man jumped out of his reach. Doing his best not to feel the sting of that rejection, Tom put his hands up in front of him and took a step back.

"Please talk to me, Joe. Tell me what's going through your mind."

"I shouldn't have done that," Joe replied anxiously, his words hitting Tom like a fist in the gut. Before he could respond, Joe shook his head and continued. "My God, you're hurt and I just... just.... What's wrong with me? I took advantage of you. It's despicable. I—"

"That's enough," Tom insisted, bringing Joe's pacing to a halt. "Nothing is wrong with you, Joe. You didn't take advantage of me. *I'm* the one who started it." His voice softened, and he couldn't help the queasy feel in his stomach when he thought about how Joe recoiled from his touch. "I'm sorry if it's not what you wanted. I didn't mean to push you into doing something you didn't want to do."

"That's not it at all. In fact it's the opposite, but... what if you have a family somewhere, kids, who are waiting for you? Starting something wouldn't be fair to any of us."

Tom gaped at him. That was certainly the last thing he expected Joe to say. "Kids?" He shook his head in disbelief, his gaze going to the couch before it came back to rest on Joe. "I think it's pretty safe to say that I don't have a spouse or kids. Jesus Christ, Joe. Do I need to remind you of what happened?" The idea of a family appealed to Tom greatly, and although he couldn't remember the people in his life, no way did he have a husband or kids, because the thought of cheating or hurting his family made him sick to his stomach.

Joe's face went up in flames, and Tom almost felt bad for him, but he wasn't about to back down now. He got the feeling Joe didn't deal with confrontation often.

"That doesn't mean you don't have someone. I won't be that guy."

"You think I'm a cheat?" Tom replied affronted. "I don't cheat, and I don't lie. The thought of cheating on someone I care about upsets me as much as it does you."

"But you don't know that," Joe insisted, tapping his head. "You can't even remember your name! What if there's someone you're crazy about who's out there frantic that you've gone missing?"

"I might not remember my name, but that doesn't mean the memories aren't in there somewhere. When I thought about someone hurting you, I felt sick to my stomach. Like I was actually going to be sick. Why would that happen, Joe? Then I think of being with someone else, and I don't feel anything. Nothing. No fuzzy images, no warmth. There's nothing there. I'm sorry if you regret what happened. I know I can't remember things, but goddammit, that doesn't mean I don't have feelings or instincts. I know deep, deep, down inside myself that I've never felt anything like what I feel when I'm around you, and not because I can't remember someone else, but because I've never felt this with anyone. It's new to me. I know it sounds crazy, but then that's pretty much the word du jour these days, but I feel like I've known you for so much longer."

"But you don't know me," Joe sighed.

"I know people. I know frustration. Before you tell me I don't know because I can't remember, I do know. I know it's important somehow, in my life, to *see* people, really see them. When I think about the world out there, bad things come to mind. Betrayal, evil, horrible human beings who care more about money than the lives they destroy. This, here, with you, it's… different."

Tom could see Joe mulling that over and becoming more wary, but he had to make Joe understand. Carefully, he walked up to Joe and gingerly took his hand, his chest tightening when Joe let him. "I'm not saying any of this to scare you, but I promised Bea I would be honest with you, Joe, and I will. Always.

Inside, I feel like I'm surrounded by darkness, but I'm not a bad person, Joe. I can't be. Not when… not when I feel like I do about you. Not when your smile feels like a lighthouse beacon, guiding me back to safe shores. I've been trapped in the shadows for so long that your light is the most amazing thing I've felt since… I don't know when. I need you. Something inside me is drawing me to you. Please don't turn me away now. Not when I've found you through the darkness."

Joe slowly pulled his hand away and closed his eyes, most likely trying to bring himself to his senses. Lord knew Tom was beginning to feel like he'd lost his. He sure as hell hoped his instincts weren't wrong about Joe. Or himself.

"I'm sorry I've caused you trouble," Tom said quietly. "When I think about it, it's crazy. Maybe it's all a bunch of bullshit." Tom's hands balled into fists at his sides. "Maybe I'm not the nice guy I tell myself I am." He looked down at his knuckles and let out a humorless laugh. "Who am I trying to kid here? Look at me. Nice guys don't live in the shadows. They don't end up facedown in the dirt, lurking in the dark with detectives looking for them."

If there hadn't been utter silence in the room, Tom would never have heard Joe's "no." He waited, holding his breath the entire time. When he thought he was going to pass out, Joe finally spoke up.

"I'm sorry. I… I don't regret what happened. I know it sounds pathetic, but this sort of thing has never been easy for me. I'm not very good at it. Relationships, I mean, not the, um, 'finding a guy with amnesia' thing. Don't think I didn't want to, because I did. I just… I've been hurt before, and by someone I knew a hell of a lot more about. It's hard for me, and it's even harder to trust someone who I don't know can be trusted."

Tom's heart squeezed at the uncertain yet endearing expression on Joe's face. The man had absolutely no idea how sweet he was. Joe had every right to tell Tom to get the hell out of his life. He had no reason to trust in anything Tom said or even listen to what Tom had to say. How could someone meet Joe and *not* fall for him?

Edging a little closer as if he were approaching a wounded animal, Tom tenderly reached out to Joe. No feelings of rejection coursed through him this time when Joe's shoulder came up a little and he stood stock-still. Tom could only imagine how much that one move must have cost Joe, who no doubt felt like running for the hills. Tom wasn't about to let Joe's bravery go unrewarded.

Pulling him into his embrace, Tom placed a kiss to Joe's temple, feeling Joe stiffen. He slowly rubbed his hand up and down Joe's back, placing little kisses on top of his head, behind his ear, his neck. Whatever the reasons for Joe's apprehensions, Tom was going to do his best to ease them. Joe needed to be cared for. Tom didn't know how he knew that. There seemed to be a lot about Joe that felt oddly… right.

"You're right," Tom admitted. "We should take things as they come, get to know each other. I know I can't tell you much, but we can still learn about each other. Maybe it'll even help me remember. Will you give me a chance to prove myself? To show you that you can trust me?"

Joe paused before relaxing in Tom's arms. He shifted from one foot to the other. "Okay."

Tom wanted to kiss Joe within an inch of his life. Instead, he said, "Deal. All right, jitterbug."

Joe met his gaze, one eyebrow arched. "What did you call me?"

Tom smiled ruefully. "Jitterbug. It seems to fit. You're all jittery and cute."

"Oh. I thought you were about to turn into George Michael and start singing."

"Would you like that?" Tom teased.

As serious as could be, Joe shook his head, but amusement shone in his eyes. "Please don't."

Tom threw his head back and laughed. Incapable of holding back, he planted a quick, sloppy kiss on Joe's lips and hugged him tight. "I wish you knew how goddamn adorable you are."

"Right, well, I should probably check on Bea and the kids. Why don't you, um, take the rest of the night off? Order us some takeout. We'll watch some TV. What do you think?"

"Sounds great." Tom headed to the couch and sat down, holding back a grin as Joe shuffled to the door, avoiding Tom's gaze like the plague. The slight flush of his cheeks gave him away, which only made the grumpy ramblings coming out of him all the more sweet.

Tom put his shirt on and sat back, thinking about everything he'd told Joe. Nothing he said hadn't been true, and a good deal of that worried him, mostly the part regarding the darkness. Whoever he was, he was all too familiar with a world so far removed from Joe's that it terrified him. He needed to remember, not just for himself, but for Joe. Whatever he was a part of, he couldn't bring that darkness down on Joe.

Chapter Six

JOE wasn't the only one smitten with Tom.

Bea had gone from being suspicious of Tom to wanting to hire him. His natural talent and skills meant she could give him any job and have it completed swiftly and efficiently. All he had to do was see how something was done once and he had it memorized. Tom strategized and executed his tasks with military precision. The kitchen had never been so spotless. Everything was fully stocked, organized, labeled, and monitored. Tom never missed a beat, and he did it all with a smile on his face and a bounce in his step. Joe had never seen anyone look so happy slicing fruit. The guy never seemed to run out of energy.

"He's like a superhero," Donnie gushed as he mopped the floor. "Did you know he can move around the kitchen with his eyes closed and not bump into anything? We tried it this morning. Didn't run into one thing. He can do pretty much anything with his eyes closed, even carve an apple! He's teaching me how to defend myself."

Joe wasn't too sure about Tom showing Donnie how to throw punches, but Donnie promised he'd be careful, and Tom wasn't wrong in believing Donnie should know how to defend himself, especially since the kid walked everywhere and was somewhat on the lanky side.

"If you like him so much, maybe you should marry him," Bea teased Donnie as she took the mop from him and handed him a tray filled with dirty dishware.

Donnie let out a snort. "If I was gay, I'd totally marry him. The guy can cook, clean, and kick butt. Admit it, Bea. You want to marry him too."

"Son, we would have been on our honeymoon by now."

"Donnie, don't encourage her," Joe muttered as he finished cleaning up the counter and came around the front. The last thing he needed was Bea going on about what she'd do to Tom on her imaginary honeymoon.

"Joe should marry him," Elsie said with a dreamy sigh. "You two would be perfect together. He's crazy about you, Joe."

Joe tripped over his feet. Luckily they'd closed shop early and there were no customers to hear this ridiculous conversation or witness another bout of gracelessness from him. More importantly, Tom was in the kitchen behind a set of thick swinging doors with some old jazz playing.

"I don't know that he's crazy about me," Joe replied, hoping his face wasn't as hot as it felt. His mind went back to the other night on the couch, and every night since then. Their evening would start out innocently enough. Dinner, some TV, maybe a movie, and then they'd somehow end up pressed together on the couch. Tom would touch Joe, and it would be all over. They'd end up half-naked giving each other hand jobs or blow jobs, with Tom making Joe's toes curl in his determination to drive Joe out of his mind. Tom's lips were magic, working Joe over, and *oh my God, why am I thinking about that now*?

"You're blushing," Elsie said with a giggle. "You know it's true."

"You know what? Get in the kitchen. Everyone in the kitchen. Mrs. Rotherford's pies won't bake themselves, and you've left Tom to do all the work."

"Well, he's like a one man pie-baking army," Donnie stated cheerfully as he left to wash the dishes. Joe shooed Bea and Elsie off to help Tom while he finished getting the shop ready for the next day. It was odd how things felt the same around here, yet different, as if Tom had always been a part of their little misfit crew. Joe knew he shouldn't think about Tom in the long term. For all they knew, Tom would wake up tomorrow and remember everything. Of course Joe wanted him to remember—he would never be so selfish as to wish Tom never regained his memory simply to have him stay—but it didn't stop Joe from worrying about what came next. Would Tom still feel the same about Joe once he stopped being Tom? Would he stop being Tom?

Bea returned from the kitchen, her pad and pencil in her hand. "Joe, I almost forgot—that friend of yours, what's his name, the one who wears all those pretty dresses?"

Joe arched an eyebrow. "Care to be more specific?"

"You know, the one who works on Broadway or something."

"Ah, Ken."

"That'd be the one. He dropped by while you popped out for groceries, said to tell you he expects you at his costume party this weekend."

"Oh, I don't know…." Joe started to grumble when Bea grabbed hold of his arm and hauled him to the other end of the room so fast he almost hurt something.

"You need to get out and have some fun, Joe. Take poor Tom with you. The man's going to go stir-crazy in there. I bet he'd love the chance to spend some time with you outside of this place."

"You really think he'd like it?" Maybe Bea was right. Just because Joe enjoyed staying in, that didn't mean the same went for Tom. Ken's penthouse was a few blocks down. If they took a cab, went straight to the party and came right back, they should be all right. Plus, it was a costume party, so Tom would be in disguise. "You're right," Joe declared, straightening and then marching into the kitchen, where Tom was kneading dough. When Tom saw him coming, the smile on his face nearly knocked Joe over, and he found himself floundering.

"Um, uh, hi, Tom."

"Everything okay?"

"Yeah, I uh, I wanted to ask if maybe, um…." Cripes, why did he turn into such a blithering idiot whenever he was faced with the man? *Just do it, Joe. For crying out loud.* He opened his mouth and the words tumbled out in a rush. "Would you like to come to a friend's costume party with me tomorrow night?"

"A party?"

Joe nodded. "I know it sounds a little crazy considering your current situation, but Ken's apartment isn't far. We take a cab there and back. You'll be in disguise. One night wouldn't hurt, right?"

Tom considered this. "Would I be going as your date?"

Joe cleared his throat. "If you're okay with that."

"Sounds like fun."

"Great. I don't generally stay very long at these things, but I thought it might be nice to go out for a while. Ken's a producer on Broadway, so he can get us some costumes. I'll give him a call tonight and ask him to get his assistant to drop them off."

"Okay."

"Okay. I'm going to uh, go make that phone call. Be back in a bit." Joe headed toward the stairs to his apartment. It was no big deal. Just because Tom was going as his date, to a party, in front of people, that was no reason to panic. It was one party. Granted, it was one of Ken's parties, but it wasn't like they had to be there long. Have a few drinks, catch up with Ken and Gordon, and say good night. It was just to get Tom out of the shop for a few hours. No big deal. Completely uneventful.

DAMN Tom and his dimples.

They were almost at penthouse level. Joe was aware of Tom trying his hardest not to smile. He hadn't stopped fidgeting since they left the apartment. The costumes had been dropped off that morning by Ken's assistant, and Tom hadn't stopped eyeing Joe since he'd put on the outfit. Ken knew Joe well, because the ringmaster costume he sent Joe covered him up pretty much from head to toe, from the black top hat on his head to his white-gloved hands and his shiny black boots. Anything more revealing would have gotten a "no" from him. Tom's outfit, on the other hand, had his legs, arms, and neck bare.

"Are you sure I don't look like an idiot?" Joe muttered, tugging on the lapels of the ornate, red tailcoat. He flicked the fringe on one of the gold shoulder epaulettes with a frown. Tom leaned in to kiss his cheek and reassure him for the hundredth time.

"You look adorable."

"Thanks. I think." Joe looked him over. "You look… wow." He still couldn't believe how amazing Tom looked. The gladiator costume fit him like a glove. The bronze-colored chest plate with rearing horses made Tom look even bigger and more imposing than usual. His muscular arms were bare except for the cuffs around his wrists, and his legs were as muscular, covered only by his sandal straps going up his calves. The costume had a lush red cape that hung from his shoulders, and a helmet with red plumes that did a good job of concealing a good portion of his face. He looked like he'd stepped off some Hollywood blockbuster set.

"You said that already," Tom chuckled. In fact Joe had said it several times, but it didn't make it any less true each time.

"Well, at least you have the legs for it. I could never pull that off. I would have skewered Ken with that plastic sword if he'd sent me a gladiator costume."

Tom looked down at himself. "I think it's a centurion."

"A what now?"

The elevator pinged and they stepped out onto the penthouse floor. There was only one door, and before Tom had a chance to reply, it swung open. A tall, slender, blond man with a wide grin and playful brown eyes stood before them in a very snug sailor's uniform. Joe looked him over before glancing at Tom and shrugging. "I thought this was a costume party?"

"You bitch!" Ken gasped before throwing himself into Joe's arms and hugging him tight. Joe laughed and returned his hug.

"Hey, Ken." Joe greeted him affectionately, allowing him to usher them into the luxurious penthouse apartment. It was packed with guests dancing, drinking, and having a good time. "Tom, this is Ken. We've known each other since high school. Ken, this is Tom."

Ken arched a perfectly shaped brow as he glanced from Joe to Tom and back. A crooked smile spread on his boyish face. *Oh, boy. Here we go.*

"We're, uh, just friends," Joe said feebly, feeling his cheeks burning.

Ken gave him a look that said he didn't believe a word of it but would wait until Joe had a few cocktails in him before the interrogation began. He turned to Tom and took his hand.

"Hello, Tom, Joe's friend."

"Hello," Tom said just as cheerfully before leaning over to whisper hoarsely, "we're more than just friends."

Joe made a strangled noise, and Ken cackled before giving Tom a big hug. "Oh, Joe, I love him already! Come on, you two. Let's get some alcohol in you. The bar's where we'll find the light of my life." He paused and gave Joe a wink. "We'll probably find Gordon there too."

Joe mumbled something under his breath as Ken led them up the stairs and out onto the roof. Joe had to admit it was stunning. The expansive roof had been transformed into a tropical paradise, from the large palms securing the guests' privacy and the exotic flower arrangements to the colorful paper lanterns glowing above their heads and cocktails served in coconuts. There were plenty of fire torches to keep the October chill away. They spotted the light of Ken's life at the large bamboo tiki bar—Gordon, not the booze. Though booze came a close second where Ken was concerned.

Gordon was a good twenty years Ken's senior, an exceptional surgeon, and as Ken stated, very much the love of his life. Just as sweet was the way Gordon doted on Ken. Joe had always admired their relationship, and at times it made him feel a little wistful. It was at least comforting to know that happily ever after did exist.

Ken leaped on Gordon, throwing his arms around the elegant man dressed like a dashing pirate, and almost made him spill his drink. Joe heard Tom chuckle beside him and turned, catching those bright silver eyes. They both gazed at each other until a look of what could easily be misconstrued as affection flashed in Tom's eyes. Joe was the first to look away. Gordon had Ken in his arms as they murmured sweetly to each other. Joe had given up some time ago on having what his friends had. Not the wealth part. Joe was never concerned with money. It wasn't their lifestyle he coveted. To Ken and Gordon, the sun and moon rose and set in their lover's eyes.

"Darling, Joe's brought a *friend*," Ken announced, snapping Joe out of his wistful thoughts. He had to get a hold of himself. This was a party, even if he wanted to groan at Ken's emphasis on the word "friend."

Gordon smiled warmly at Joe and gave him a firm handshake, his hazel eyes filled with amusement. "Joe, it's so nice to see you again. It's been too long."

"I know. I'm sorry. You know how time gets away from me when I'm at the shop. Gordon, this is Tom."

"Joe's friend," Ken pitched in. In case anyone had forgotten in the last ten seconds. Gordon shook Tom's hand, and Joe took the opportunity to lean behind Gordon and stick his tongue out at the chipper sailor. Ken just laughed.

"It's a pleasure to meet you both," Tom said with a broad grin.

Joe noticed Ken's hand subtly disappear behind his lover's back. Gordon turned to Joe.

"Joe, I've got a couple of friends I want you to meet. They work in my hospital and just about need resuscitating every time I bring one of your pies in. They'd love to meet you." He turned to Ken and gave his cheek a peck. "Why don't you get Tom a drink, darling?"

"Of course." Ken smiled and returned his lover's kiss before taking Tom's arm.

Did they really think Joe didn't know what they were up to? Subtlety was not a part of Ken's vocabulary. Before Joe could utter a word, Ken had whisked Tom away. It would be fine. Maybe if Joe told himself that enough times, he might actually believe it.

THE moment Gordon and Joe were out of earshot, Ken pounced. "You won't try and hide anything from me, will you?"

Tom turned his gaze away from Joe to smile at Ken. "That was quite smooth. Years of practice?"

"Are you kidding? Finding your way around Joe is like trying to find your way through a maze blindfolded, while moving backward, with your ankles bound together. In a storm."

Tom laughed. "That sounds about right." His smile faded and he couldn't help the soft sigh that escaped him. "Someone hurt him pretty bad."

Ken led Tom over to one of the smaller bars and they put in their orders. "Joe told you?"

"He won't talk about it. I just know something happened that really hurt him. Every time I think he's starting to let me in, he pulls away." Someone had really done a number on Joe, but Tom didn't want to pry or push.

Ken nodded somberly. "When Joe's ready, he'll tell you."

"I wish there was something I could do to make Joe understand I would never hurt him. I really care about him." He took a sip of his drink. Man, he needed to lighten up. This was a party, one he was attending with Joe. Not the time to be sulking. "So how did you and Gordon meet?"

"You'd never believe it, but I ended up on his operating table. I was rushed to the hospital after suffering from appendicitis. I remember being in so much pain and then blacking out. When I woke up, the surgeon was there, and I thought I'd died and gone to heaven. There he was, standing over me. The most gorgeous man I'd ever met." Ken sighed and twirled the little umbrella in his drink. "He saved me twice that day."

"That's got to be the sweetest thing ever. Next to Joe, that is."

Ken clamped a hand over his mouth to contain his delighted giggle. Managing to compose himself, he leaned in close. "You more than just care about him, don't you?"

"Oh?" Tom asked.

"You should know that Joe has *never*, and I do mean never, brought anyone to any of our parties. Ever.

I really didn't expect him to come, much less ask for two costumes. That says a lot, believe me. Tell me. What's Joe said to you?"

"This is Joe we're talking about, remember?" Tom mumbled. "He's just…."

"Stubborn? Pigheaded? Wouldn't know love if it came shimmying down the drainpipe with neon signs and trumpets blaring? If he did actually recognize it, would then think he didn't deserve it and try to run from here to Timbuktu?"

"Wow, you really do know him well. I think he cares about me. He's been amazing. It feels right, being with him. But if I get too close, he bolts."

"Wow." Ken whistled. "He has got it bad."

"So… running away is a good thing?" If that was the case, then Joe was nuts about him.

"Joe has a habit of letting his emotions run away with him, but he's good at covering it up when it happens. It's all part of that goofy charm of his. The idea of being in love scares the hell out of him, which is understandable, but someone has to teach him that if he doesn't take a risk, he'll never get what he wants. Everyone's got buttons. Even Joe. We just need to find the right one and push it."

Tom studied Ken warily. The look on his face made him a little nervous. He looked like a cat ready to pounce. "Oh?"

"Don't you worry, handsome. I know Joe better than Joe knows himself." He spotted Joe still chatting to Gordon, then looked toward the other end of the roof. "Tom, I'd like to introduce you to someone. Well, some*ones*." He grabbed Tom's hand and led him across the roof to a group of young men, flirting and tasting each other's cocktails.

"Boys," Ken purred, getting the attention of the five pretty young men—all of whom looked to be in their twenties. They were dressed in Greek togas. "Tom, meet the Brooklyn Brats."

"Hello," Tom said nervously as five blond heads and five pairs of sparkling blue eyes all turned simultaneously toward him, their pink lips smiling widely.

"They're brothers," Ken whispered. "They're also scandalous, hell on earth, notoriously flirty, and *love* a good soldier. Have fun."

Before Tom could utter a word, Ken was gone and the five blonds were devouring him with their eyes before slowly circling him.

So, this is what it feels like to be thrown to the lions.

JOE finished telling Ken and Gordon about the circumstances surrounding Tom's sudden appearance in his life, making sure to leave out the parts with the men looking for Tom. He trusted his friends wholeheartedly. Not only were they good people, but they fussed over him as much as Bea and the kids, if not more so. Joe felt guilty for not keeping in touch as much as he wanted. He had a habit of hiding away in his own little world.

"If I were you, I'd take that as a sign," Ken said with a grin. He took another sip of his cocktail, a mischievous look in his eyes.

"Yeah, a sign that you need help," Joe grumbled, tightening his hands around the whip. He was grateful for the prop. He wouldn't have known what to do with his hands otherwise, seeing as his pants had no pockets. Well, fake pockets. What was it with clothes and fake pockets? What was the point? They were deceptive, and evil. "You're suggesting I shack up with a guy I found outside my doorstep because he's good-looking." Not that he'd been doing less scandalous things with Tom already, but his friends certainly didn't have to know that.

Ken waved his concerns away. "Don't be silly. He's not just a gorgeous man you found on your doorstep. He's Tom. You've been living with him for a few weeks now, spending all day and night with him. So what if you don't know where he's from or what his job is? What's it matter compared to having someone completely crazy about you?"

Joe choked on his drink, then murmured, "Thank you," to Gordon for the napkin to wipe the dribble off his chin. Classy. "Who said he's crazy about me?"

Ken shrugged.

"No, Ken, no—" He mimicked Ken's shrug. "Use words. Words that make sense to normal people like me and Gordon." That got a snort from Ken.

"Normal? Honey, normal people don't stick their heads in household appliances. Besides, who wants to be normal when you can have a Roman centurion?"

"When did everyone become such an expert in Roman history?" Joe frowned. At the puzzled expressions he sighed. "I thought he was a gladiator."

Gordon shook his head. "Gladiators were combatants. Centurion's had the helmets with the plumes. They were officers of the Roman armies."

Joe was uninspired. "Thanks, professor. I'll make sure to brush up on my history lesson before the next costume party." He'd started to open his mouth when he heard a gaggle of laughter and titters erupt from the corner of the roof. Craning his neck around Ken, his jaw nearly unhinged at the sight of the Brooklyn Brats all over Tom. "When the hell did he become such a social butterfly?"

"Hmm?" Ken casually turned to see what Joe was scowling at. "Looks like he's quite the catch. They're practically throwing themselves at his feet."

"Among other things," Joe grunted, his eyes narrowing at the spectacle. "Those little hussies! Look at them. They're shameless." One blond Adonis was hanging on to Tom's left bicep. Another was tugging at the hem of his tunic. A third was running his fingers through the helmet's plumes and giggling. The fourth was wrapping himself in Tom's cape, and the fifth wasn't bothering with any subtlety at all as he ran his finger slowly down the faux sword attached to Tom's belt. The man himself seemed to be completely unawares, standing there chatting away. My God, he couldn't be that oblivious. Could he? "Someone should save him."

"Maybe he doesn't want saving," Gordon mused. "Most men don't when caught in their clutches. After all, they're very picky about their prey. Everyone knows they only sink their teeth into the best meat."

Joe shot him a glare. "Tom's not meat, and he's not interested in becoming their prey, either. Besides," he purred, fluttering his lashes, "he's crazy about me."

"Maybe he's tired of waiting for you to reciprocate?" Ken countered most nonchalantly, his eyes everywhere but on Joe.

"What do you mean?" Joe asked, feeling the blood drain from his face.

"Well, I mean, the man might not remember who he is, but surely you don't expect him to wait around for you forever, do you? He might meet someone else who doesn't find his lack of identity a problem and steal him from you."

"Well, considering he's not mine to begin with, they wouldn't be stealing," Joe said haughtily, though his heart was fighting him on that one. What if Tom really was waiting for him? He was always so sweet and affectionate, always the one to initiate things. Sometimes he thought maybe Tom did it because he was grateful to Joe, but the more he thought about it, the less he believed that. From the very beginning, Tom wore his heart on his sleeve, always being open and honest with Joe.

"So you're just going to let the lions have him? If they don't finish him off, I guarantee there are a few more vultures circling at the moment."

Sure enough, when Joe scanned the rooftop, there were at least six or seven more men waiting for their chance at Tom. God, it was like a feeding frenzy. It wasn't so much the thought of them ogling Tom—because frankly it was hard not to notice the man—but the thought of someone waltzing in and taking Joe's place in Tom's heart, all because he was too much of a coward to take a chance. Taking a deep breath, Joe tilted his top hat back and gave it a firm pat before making straight for the lions.

"All right, beat it," he growled, shooing the disgruntled youths away and grabbing Tom by the waist, pulling him hard against him. Tom's eyes widened and he flushed, sending a tingle up Joe's spine. Joe crushed his mouth to Tom's and kissed him hard, claiming him right there in front of everyone.

For a moment Tom appeared too stunned to move. He was probably wondering if Joe had done what he thought he'd done. Joe couldn't believe what he was doing, but all further thought fled from his mind as he kissed Tom heatedly and thoroughly. It was only when they were forced to come up for air that Joe saw the look of raw desire in Tom's eyes, and it sent a shudder through him.

"I thought you wouldn't come for me."

"You thought wrong," Joe said, sounding breathless. An "oomph!" escaped him when Tom brought Joe up hard against him, kissing him deeply. It was only when Joe felt someone give his coat a gentle tug that he realized Ken and Gordon were trying to get their attention.

"As thrilled as we are, boys," Ken said, beaming, "you're making the natives restless. Not to mention, very, very jealous."

Tom laughed shyly, and Joe, who'd only just realized what he'd done in front of everyone, wrapped his arms around Tom's waist, and buried his face against his neck.

Ken's eyes danced with amusement. "Well, it's better than an oven."

Joe glared at Ken, who cackled as he walked off, and the DJ began to play a soft romantic ballad.

Tom slipped his hands around Joe's waist and started to sway, his voice laced with amusement when he said, "Since we're already here, how about a dance?"

Joe put on his big boy pants and pulled back to meet Tom's eyes. The man really was handsome. "I'd like that."

"Thank you for coming to my rescue," Tom said, taking Joe's hand in his and placing the other on Joe's waist. They swayed slowly in time to the music. Joe couldn't remember the last time he'd slow danced with someone. Had it been prom?

"Well, you *are* my date. I could hardly leave you to become their dinner, though you didn't look all that alarmed." Joe narrowed his eyes, ignoring the way his lip twitched, clearly eager to smile.

"I was trying to be polite. The experience was quite traumatizing, actually." Tom pouted, and Joe went along with it.

"Was it now?"

"Yep. I think maybe I might need some soothing." Tom brought Joe in a little closer and gave him a soft kiss. "Maybe some of this…." He brushed his lips over Joe's for a feathery kiss before moving his lips to Joe's jaw. "Maybe a little of this…." He nipped at Joe's jawline, his voice low and husky. "Maybe a few more drinks, a little mingling, and we find ourselves a little privacy where we can… reassure each other."

Joe all but melted against Tom. "I think that can be arranged." He couldn't believe his boldness, but he took Tom's hand and led him back to the stairs leading to the apartment. Joe bit on his bottom lip, hoping Ken wouldn't mind—not that he would, really, but still. Was he going to do this? Joe refused to give it any more thought. He hurried through the apartment to the large linen closet at the end of the hall past the guest bathroom. Making sure no one saw him, he opened it, then pushed Tom inside before following him in. He turned on the light and closed the door behind them. There was plenty of room.

"Joe, what—"

Joe cut Tom off with a kiss. He couldn't let himself think too much or he'd get cold feet. He'd never done anything like this before. Lucky for them, Joe didn't have to worry about Tom's pants, considering he wasn't wearing any. Joe got on his knees, and Tom sucked in his breath. Joe lifted the lower half of Tom's costume.

"Hold that."

"Okay."

Joe couldn't help but chuckle at Tom's eager acceptance. As a reward, Joe pulled down Tom's black boxer briefs, freeing his already half-hard shaft. It was as amazing as the first time he'd seen it. The man was gorgeous all over, and all Joe wanted to do was taste him.

With a smile, Joe took hold of Tom's erection and drew it into his mouth, moaning around Tom's length. Tom bucked his hips and threw a hand out to the side, grabbing a fistful of the shelved towels as Joe proceeded to suck, lick, and nip Tom's erection. He started off slow, loving the taste of Tom, the scent of shower gel and his musk. Joe held the base of Tom's cock as he pulled off him and pressed the tip of his tongue to Tom's slit.

"Oh God, Joe…."

Tom's plea resulted in Joe doubling his efforts. He picked up his pace, keeping his lips pressed tight around Tom as he moved up to the tip, where he worked his tongue around the head before he moved back down, making a meal out of Tom. He popped off Tom long enough to wet his finger before sucking Tom down again. With his wet digit, he carefully pushed it against Tom's hole, moaning when Tom gasped and thrust his hips up. Joe swallowed Tom almost down to the root and allowed Tom to take hold of his head and thrust his hips, sliding himself in and out.

"Joe, I'm going to come."

Joe responded to Tom's breathless declaration by pushing his finger further into Tom and crooking his finger.

Tom gritted his teeth as he cried out, spilling himself inside Joe's mouth. Joe swallowed down every drop, moving his hand to Tom's leg as Tom doubled over and held on to Joe's head until he was spent. Joe stood and cupped the back of Tom's head. Tom gazed dreamily, his silver eyes sparkling with need, want, and something that made Joe's heart skip a beat. He leaned in and kissed Tom, slipping his tongue inside Tom's mouth so he could taste himself. Tom groaned and his knees wobbled. Joe pulled back and nipped at Tom's bottom lip.

"How's that for soothing?"

Chapter Seven

ANOTHER great day.

The café had been busy as usual, and everyone worked hard. Of course there may have been a little play in between. Ever since Ken and Gordon's party, it was difficult for Joe and Tom to keep their hands off each other. With a sigh, Joe finished turning the chairs over and placing them on the tables. Just his luck. After all these years, he'd finally found a guy who he could possibly have a future with, and the man had amnesia. Then again, what were the chances of a man like Tom even noticing Joe if he hadn't ended up unconscious in his garden?

Squeals, giggling, and laughter filtered in through the kitchen doors. What on earth? Joe finished up and pushed through the swinging doors just as Donnie whizzed by and a handful of flour smacked Joe in the face. Eyes shut, he stood serenely.

"Joe, I'm so sorry. Keep your eyes closed." Tom gently blew on Joe's face then dabbed at his skin with a wet paper towel. When it was safe, Joe opened his eyes. He arched an eyebrow at Tom, who was doing his best not to laugh. He was failing quite spectacularly. "I'm sorry. I really am."

"And here I thought Bea and Donnie were the ones needing supervision."

Donnie and Bea both protested simultaneously. "Hey."

Joe shook his head at Bea in shame. "Aren't you a little mature for this?"

Bea lifted her chin in defiance. "Even I know when to have a little fun."

What was this now? "You're saying I don't know how to have fun?" He knew how to have fun. He couldn't think of any examples at the moment, but he could have fun.

"Prove it." Bea took his hand and poured a load of flour onto it. Joe was less than inspired.

"I don't have to prove it. And these are my ingredients you're tossing about willy-nilly."

Bea pursed her lips and chucked another handful of flour at his face. "That's for saying willy-nilly. No grown man says that."

"I say it, and I'm a grown man," Joe protested, wiping the flour from his face.

"That's debatable," Donnie replied with a giggle.

Joe gasped. "Et tu?" He pointed behind Donnie. "Is that a spider?"

"Where?" Donnie turned around. "I don't see it." He turned back to Joe and got floured.

Joe grinned smugly. "Debate *that*."

He should have known better. Everyone peered at each other before they launched into an attack. More flour floated through the air than, well, air. It was snowing down, covering them from head to toe, except for Tom. Tom was a little too clean, so Joe decided to enlist the help of his enemies. He caught Donnie's attention and motioned toward Tom. Donnie enlisted Elsie, who then recruited Bea. The four of them grabbed a handful of four and set their sights on Tom.

"Oh, I see how it is." Tom narrowed his eyes as he backed away. "Gang up on the new guy."

"Someone has to take the fall, Tom, and you're too darn good." Joe had prepared to launch his attack when Tom pulled some super spy move and ended up with his arms around Joe before he knew what hit him. He let out a yelp as Tom lifted him off his feet, the flour in his hand falling away as he was thrown over Tom's shoulder. Joe couldn't stop himself from laughing. "Put me down!"

Tom turned to Bea, Donnie, and Elsie. "All right. Lower your flour or the cute guy gets it."

"Hm." Bea seemed to be considering this.

Joe peered at her from over his shoulder. "You're taking awfully long saving me, Bea."

"I'm considering my options."

"What options? You're supposed to drop the flour and come to my rescue!"

"What'll it cost him if we don't surrender?" Bea asked.

Tom smacked Joe's butt, and Joe let out another yelp. "You scoundrel!" Joe wriggled and pushed against Tom's back, coming up against nothing but muscle. Damn the man and his finely sculpted figure.

Nice view, though. Very nice indeed. Tom had a perky round butt, and Joe had the strongest urge to squeeze it, but he restrained himself. He really shouldn't molest Tom in front of everyone.

Tom thought about his reply. "It'll cost him… a kiss."

"Extortion!" Joe declared. "What kind of kiss?"

"I'll decide once you accept," Tom replied cheerfully.

Joe pretended to think about it. "Well, I suppose I can afford one kiss, and of course, I'm hardly in the position to refuse. You drive a hard bargain."

Tom chuckled and put Joe on his feet, a wicked gleam coming into his eyes. "I get to claim the kiss." He took hold of Joe and bent him backward, kissing him within an inch of his life, while their friends cheered and made catcalls behind them. Joe wrapped his arms around Tom's neck and returned his kiss. He never wanted this moment to end. Being in Tom's arms—feeling his lips against Tom's, the taste of him, experiencing the need coming from Tom—was heavenly. Unfortunately it did end, interrupted by a knock on the glass door out front. Tom pulled Joe up and let out a breathy laugh. "It's probably a good thing they interrupted us, or we might have ended up giving everyone quite the show." Tom wriggled his eyebrows, and Joe put a hand to Tom's chest.

"Restrain yourself, sir. We are in the presence of gentlefolk. And Bea."

Bea huffed and took a step toward Joe. "Why you—"

With a laugh, Joe darted from the kitchen. He couldn't remember the last time he'd had so much fun. Joe wiped his hands on his apron and headed out into the café. With the blinds closed on all the windows and the front door shade pulled down, he couldn't get a good look at who was on the other side. Joe opened the door and his smile fell from his face. His heart dropped to his stomach.

"Hey, Joe. Long time no see."

Joe swallowed hard, unable to believe it. "Blake? What are you doing here?"

"Is that any way to greet a customer? Where's the warm and friendly service I hear so much about?" Blake gave him a wide toothy grin. At one point that smile and those chocolate brown eyes had sent tingles up Joe's spine. Now they made him feel sick. To think he'd fallen for that soulless gaze. How could he have been so naïve, to ever believe the man loved him? The only man Blake ever loved was himself.

"What do you want, Blake?"

Blake straightened to his full height as he had a habit of doing around those he believed himself better than. His smile didn't reach his eyes, and he turned his nose up slightly. "I'll cut to the chase. You're catering Alecia Rotherford's party, and I can't be outdone by that new money trash. I'm having a party next weekend, and I want you to cater it."

Joe stared at him. Well, didn't that just beat all? The man was out of his mind. He leaned out the door and looked up at the sky.

"What are you looking at?" Blake asked with a frown.

"Flying pigs. Nope. Don't see any." Joe turned his attention back to Blake. "You're kidding, right?"

"Oh come on, Joe. That was years ago. Surely you can't still be upset." Blake leaned in and brushed some flour out of Joe's hair. He took the opportunity to whisper in Joe's ear. "You still look good, Joe."

Joe's blood boiled. The absolute nerve of the guy! "Are you serious?" The painful memories flooded back, washing over Joe and leaving him nearly shaking with anger. "I was in a coma for days! I was almost killed. Then to add insult to injury, you told your father I tried to sexually assault you! How could you do that to me? You took everything from me! My shop, my savings, my apartment, my reputation…."

"Hey, that wasn't my fault. My father was the one who did all that."

"And what did *you* do?" Joe demanded. "You did nothing! You said you loved me but you let him destroy me, destroy everything I'd worked so hard for."

Blake shrugged. "In my defense, it wasn't really all that much, Joe. Besides, if I'd told him the truth, he would have cut me off, and then we would have both been on the street. I had far more to lose than you." His expression softened, and he put his hand to Joe's cheek. "We had some good times, didn't we? Remember our first Valentine's Day at the Hilton?"

Joe remembered. It was the day Joe had fallen for Blake, believing everything Blake did for him that day had been because he cared. The limo that picked Joe up, the fancy hotel room filled with red roses and champagne. Blake turned down several invitations to extravagant parties to spend the night with Joe. They watched movies, laughed, and made love. Joe had never been happier, or more delusional.

"I remember," Joe said quietly. "But that doesn't make up for what happened after."

Blake sighed. "You had to know it wouldn't work out between us. I have a legacy to uphold. As the only heir, I was always going to have a wife, and have her children. You know my family, Joe. No one breaks with tradition. Does that mean I shouldn't get what I need? You should be thanking me, really. If I had asked you to stay, you would have. And instead of this," Blake motioned around him, "you would have had a penthouse and spending account. You wouldn't have been happy."

Joe couldn't believe what he was hearing. Tears sprang in his eyes, and he quickly blinked them away. He wouldn't give the bastard the satisfaction.

"So how much will it take?" Blake removed his wallet and took out a wad of cash, then put it in Joe's hand. "Come on, Joe. You can use the money. Get some furniture for this place from this century."

Joe threw the money in Blake's face. "Get out of my shop, you son of a bitch."

"Now listen here, you pathetic little nobody. I—"

Blake was cut off by Tom punching him square across the jaw. He reeled back, falling into the doorframe. Joe stood stunned, the murderous glare coming from Tom giving him pause. Blake scrambled to his feet and took a step forward. He came to a halt when something in Tom's gaze and stance told him he better consider his next move very carefully. Tom's silver eyes were hard as steel, his jaw clenched tight, and his hands curled into fists at his sides. He looked lethal, and certainly not a man to be trifled with. Joe had never seen this side of Tom. Was this a hint of the man who lay underneath?

"He said get the hell out." Tom's voice was low and grave, his warning less than subtle.

Blake straightened out his suit and glared at them. "This isn't over. You'll be hearing from my firm."

Tom took a step toward Blake who took a step back. "I'll be waiting."

Blake quickly gathered up his discarded bills and stomped out of the shop. Tom locked up behind him. His expression softened the moment he turned to Joe.

"Are you okay?"

Joe opened his mouth to reply but nothing came out. He shook his head, trying his hardest to keep his emotions in check. After all these years, why the hell did the guy have to come back? He'd been doing so well, and now…. Oh God, what if it happened all over again?

"Excuse me." Joe was finding it hard to breathe. He needed air. The garden. That always helped. Joe hurried out the side door into the garden and the cool night air. It couldn't happen again. He couldn't go through that a second time. Everything had been going so well. For the first time in a long time, it seemed like he was moving on with his life. Things were good. He was happy. Why now? Wasn't once enough? Joe sat on the stone bench, unable to keep the tears at bay any longer.

TOM stood in the middle of the café wondering what to do next. Should he go after Joe? He wanted to, but he didn't want to impose on Joe's privacy. If he could, he'd go after that bastard and teach him a thing or two about manners. Whoever he was—aside from being a complete and utter asshole—he'd really upset Joe. He heard them arguing, but only walked in to see Joe throw the guy's money back at him and tell him to leave. Tom had never seen Joe so angry. He'd seen Joe frustrated or annoyed, but he had an amazing way of picking himself up, of looking at the bright side of things.

"You should go to him," Bea said quietly. The pain in her kind eyes squeezed at Tom's heart.

"Who was that guy?"

"It's not my place to say. Only Joe can tell you that." She patted his arm and headed for the kitchen.

"We'll clean up and close the shop. He needs you, Tom, more than he's willing to admit."

Tom took Bea's advice and walked out into the garden, finding Joe sitting on the stone bench, his face turned up to the sky and his eyes glassy. When Joe spotted him, he quickly wiped at his eyes. Tom sat beside him and took Joe's hand in his, stroking Joe's skin with his thumb.

"Talk to me, Joe. Who was that?"

"That was my ex."

Tom's eyebrows shot up toward his hairline. Ex? Never in a million years would he have imagined Joe with a jerk like that. The guy clearly had a lot of money, but Tom didn't think for a moment that Joe had been with the man because of that. If Joe had been with him, it meant he cared about the guy at some point.

"We were together years ago. He was still in college, and I'd finally saved up enough to buy my first shop. It was a great little place down in the Village, a couple of blocks away from my apartment. Blake wasn't out. He couldn't be. His family's extremely wealthy. When we met, he was such a nice guy, or at least that's what I thought. It was tough having to hide, but I understood. I didn't have anyone, but he had a family, and his father was a court judge, high up the food chain." Joe let out a shuddered sigh, and it nearly broke Tom's heart.

"Blake invited me to spend the night. His father was down at the Hamptons and wouldn't be back until the end of the weekend. One night, we were together in bed and his father walked in on us."

Tom kept himself from cursing. He had the sneaking suspicion it didn't go well.

"Blake panicked. His father would cut him off without a penny and throw him out into the streets if he thought Blake was gay, so Blake did what he does best. He protected himself and threw me under the bus. He told his father he invited me over to study, that I drugged him and tried to force him to have sex. He made me sound like… like some kind of monster."

Tom clenched his jaw to keep himself from saying anything, namely cursing the bastards to high heaven, especially Blake the weasel.

"I left as quickly as I could. The next night I was walking home from the shop and I got jumped by a group of men. They beat the hell out of me. That's how I met Bea. It was in front of her house. She heard the commotion and called the cops. Lucky for me, an officer was on patrol nearby, and he rushed to my aid. If it wasn't for him, I probably wouldn't be here now. I was in an induced coma for days."

Tom was having trouble believing what he just heard. "Jesus, Joe." He wanted to go back out there and find that son of a bitch Blake and see how well he liked getting the life beat out of him. His anger rose, a familiar sickness unsettling his stomach when he thought about Joe bloodied and broken on the street. If there was a monster in this story, it wasn't Joe. Sweet, kind Joe, who always had a smile and a kind word for everyone. Tom took several deep breaths to calm himself.

"When I woke up, the nurses told me the name of the officer who saved me, and how he came to visit me every day after his shift. He found out I didn't have anybody, so he stayed with me every night. He'd talk to me and play soft music. He was gone by the time I was conscious enough to remember more than someone placing ice chips to my lips. I tried to find him, to thank him, but he transferred out of state," Joe said with a sigh.

"Wherever he is, I'm sure he knows how much you appreciate what he did." Tom was happy to hear Joe hadn't been alone. He brought Joe's hand to his lips for a kiss. If only he'd known Joe at the time. He would have been there at his side. Maybe it was for the best he hadn't been around, or he might have hunted Blake down and done something stupid.

"It's probably for the best. I don't know how I would have faced him, knowing how I'd ended up there. The guy probably thought I was an idiot. I sure as hell felt like one. I thought Blake loved me. I was so stupid. If getting beat up wasn't enough, whatever didn't get eaten by the hospital bills was lost in the lawsuit. Blake's assault charges never stuck because of the lack of evidence, but it was enough to drag my name through the mud. I lost my shop, my apartment, everything. I was on the street, and funny enough ended up in front of Bea's house again. She took me in and looked after me until I could get back on my feet. When her husband died, she needed to keep herself busy. By then I'd opened Apple'n, Pies, so I offered her a job." Joe pulled away, fear in his blue-green eyes. "What if Blake goes through with his threat? I can't lose it all again, Tom, I can't…."

"Listen to me, Joe. You weren't stupid. You put your trust in someone you cared about, someone you thought cared about you. What happened wasn't your fault. You're a wonderful, gentle man who deserved so much better." Tom held him close and kissed the top of his head. "I promise I won't let anything happen to you. I don't care how much money Blake and his family has. I won't let him hurt you again."

Joe clung to Tom, digging his fingers into Tom's back, and burying his face against Tom's neck, a whispered

"Thank you" slipping from Joe's lips. They sat there for what seemed like ages, holding on to each other. The night grew chilly, and Joe took Tom's hand. He stood and pulled Tom along with him, leading him upstairs to his apartment. Tom allowed Joe to take the lead, standing to one side as Joe locked the door, then cupped Tom's face, drawing him in for a heated kiss.

Joe's kiss was filled with need and desire, one that stoked the fire inside Tom. A shiver went through him as Joe slipped his hands under Tom's T-shirt, caressing and exploring, his boldness growing by the moment. Their breaths mingled, and Joe pressed himself against Tom, the feel of their erections rubbing causing Tom to let out a low groan. He'd never wanted anything so badly in all his life. How he knew that was beyond him, but he could feel it down to the depths of his soul.

"Tom," Joe pleaded, pulling back enough to meet Tom's gaze, the heat in his eyes setting Tom ablaze. "I need you."

"Are you sure?"

"There's not a lot I've been sure of in my life, but this—" Joe pressed his lips to Tom's for another fiery kiss before pulling back. "This I'm sure of."

Tom didn't need to hear more. They scrambled to undress each other, dropping items of clothing on the way to the bedroom. Tom kissed Joe as if he were trying to consume him. When he had Joe naked, he gently pushed him back onto the bed. "Please tell me you have supplies."

"Nightstand," Joe breathed, moving to the middle of the bed. Tom was on his heels. He turned on the small lamp on the nightstand and rummaged through the drawer, grabbing what he needed, then dropped them beside him on the bed. Tom paused long enough to admire Joe and his gorgeous body.

"Joe, you're amazing."

Joe's bashfulness was endearing. "How do you see things no one else does?"

"You're the one who doesn't see it, Joe, but I'm going to show you." How could Joe not know how beautiful he was? Tom ran his hands from Joe's shoulders to his chest, down his torso. His soft skin was flushed from his cheeks to the tips of his ears down to his shoulders. Tom could get lost in those blue-green eyes. He bent over and kissed Joe, loving the sweet taste of his mouth. The rest of Joe was just as sweet.

Tom trailed kisses down Joe's neck to his chest, taking a moment to lavish some affection on Joe's pink nipples, relishing in the little noises Joe made as Tom licked the pebbled nubs. Joe arched his back, and Tom continued his journey of exploration. He nipped at Joe's skin and gently scraped his fingernails until Joe writhed beneath him.

"Please, Tom."

Tom placed a pillow under Joe's hips before taking hold of the lube. He smiled when he saw it was cherry scented. Joe's blush intensified and Tom couldn't wait anymore. He kept his eyes on Joe as he rolled the condom onto his shaft, then pressed his lubed fingers to Joe's entrance. Joe's gasp was music to Tom's ears, and he had to force himself to take it slow. As soon as Joe was ready, Tom leaned in to kiss Joe and replaced his fingers with his rock-hard erection. Gingerly he pushed himself inside Joe, inch by excruciating inch. Joe moaned and arched his back. He wrapped his legs around Tom and pulled him down against him. They brought their lips together in another heated kiss as Tom began to move. His muscles strained as he pulled out slowly nearly to the tip and leisurely pushed himself back in down to the root.

"Tom," Joe pleaded.

Tom did his best to drive Joe crazy. He rained kisses on his neck and up his jaw before taking Joe's earlobe between his teeth. He picked up his pace a little, taking hold of Joe's hand and lacing their fingers together while he took hold of Joe's cock with his free hand, pumping his fist slowly to match his thrusts. Their skin was warm and beaded with sweat as they lay pressed together. Joe let his head fall back, exposing his neck, and Tom took advantage. His nipped, kissed, and licked at Joe's delicious skin.

"Please, Tom."

Tom snapped his hips, smiling when Joe let out a surprised gasp. He writhed underneath Tom, his whimpers and murmurs for Tom to give him more sending a shiver through him. Tom obliged, giving Joe exactly what he wanted. He moved Joe's hand to his cock so he could take over the task while Tom sat back and took hold of Joe's legs, pushing them up against his chest. Tom never took his eyes off Joe as he pushed himself deeper and harder with each thrust, his pace quickening, fueled by Joe's sweet moans and gasps of pleasure.

Their breathing grew ragged, and Tom buried himself deep in Joe, thrilled by the tightness around him and the ecstasy on Joe's face as he threw out a hand to grab a fistful of the bedsheets. His stomach muscles tightened, and Tom knew Joe was close.

"Come for me, Joe."

Joe pumped his fist, losing his rhythm just as Tom did. He was so damned gorgeous, his lips wet and parted as he came. The sight was enough to send Tom hurtling toward his own release, and he smacked his hips against Joe's ass, his teeth clenched as his orgasm burst free as he pumped into Joe. He bent over and kissed Joe as they rode out their orgasms until they were both too sensitive. Tom carefully pulled out of Joe. He kissed Joe slow and deep before removing the condom and tying it off. He threw it away in the small wastebasket by the rolltop desk on the side of the room.

Joe got under the covers and held them up for Tom as he slid in behind Joe, pulling Joe back against him. They spooned, and Tom smiled before placing a kiss to Joe's shoulder. It was strange. He felt like he'd been waiting for this for a long time. It didn't make any sense. No, actually it was the only thing in his life that made sense right now. He should be worried or frustrated that he couldn't remember anything, but being here with Joe in his arms somehow made everything less frightening. He put his hand against Joe's chest, over his heart, and Joe hummed a lovely little melody Tom was certain he'd heard before. Like everything else he tried to remember, it was fuzzy, in the distance and just out of his reach, but it was there. Tom couldn't place it, but it meant something to him. It was important.

Tom closed his eyes and nuzzled his face against Joe's hair. Whether he regained his memory or not, it wouldn't replace the ones he was making with Joe. It wouldn't change the way his pulse sped up when Joe entered the room, or the way his heart skipped a beat when Joe smiled at him. Whatever happened, he was lucky to have found Joe, and he had no intention of letting him go.

Chapter Eight

JOE woke up with a smile on his face. He couldn't seem to get rid of it. Not that he wanted to, at least until he rolled over and found the bed empty. His heart sank and all kinds of troubling thoughts came into his head.

Usually Tom was still asleep at this time. Joe tried his best not to panic. Did Tom regret what they'd done? Maybe sometime in the middle of the night Tom had woken up, memory intact, and run off to his old life wondering what the heck had possessed him to shack up with a guy like Joe.

Joe got up and dressed, though not before giving himself a good talking-to. He needed to have more faith in Tom. His friends were right: he couldn't let that jerk Blake ruin his chances for a future, whether that future involved Tom or not. With each passing day it was getting harder to ignore his heart or the way his stomach filled with butterflies every time Tom smiled at him. Tom was handsome, strong, with a smile that could outshine the brightest star. It wasn't just the sex, though that had been amazing. Every muscle in Joe's body ached in the most delicious way, and the thought of Tom had Joe smiling like a dope.

After his morning routine, he dressed and headed into the kitchen. The mouthwatering scents of frying bacon and aromatic coffee had him all but floating into the kitchen, where he found Tom. His bright smile lit up the room, and it tugged at something inside Joe. What might it be like to wake up every morning to that smile?

"Morning, sunshine. Why don't you have a seat?" Tom motioned over to the breakfast nook, and Joe happily obliged. No man had ever made him breakfast before. He certainly hadn't expected the spread Tom laid before him: scrambled eggs, sausage links, bacon, hash browns, buttered toast, fluffy homemade pancakes with strawberry compote, maple syrup, coffee, and in a tiny blue vase, a flower from the garden. Breakfast smelled heavenly, but when Tom walked over and kissed him, Joe was floating high.

"You didn't have to do all this," Joe said, thanking Tom when he handed Joe a large mug of coffee. Joe took a sip and moaned. It was exactly the way he liked it: a little bit of milk and two sugars.

"I wanted to," Tom replied with a wink. He took a seat across from Joe and poured himself some coffee. "You deserve to be pampered a little, Joe. You work so hard."

Joe didn't quite know what to say to that. He'd thrown himself into his work since opening the new café downstairs. It was smaller than the first one, and a little behind the times, but he'd worked day and night to turn it into what it was now. Maybe he didn't have the money for renovations, but the café was doing exceptionally well. If he continued to save and maybe took a small risk, he could afford the renovations; start small. He didn't know where the notion came from, but it didn't seem as daunting as it once had.

Now that he thought about it, he couldn't remember the last time he'd taken a vacation. He didn't know why he was thinking of these things now. He loved what he did, so time off wasn't something he ever felt he needed. Then again, it had been a long time since he had anyone to enjoy a vacation with.

As they sat and had breakfast together, Joe couldn't help but ask. "How are you doing, Tom?"

Tom glanced up from his coffee and paper. "How do you mean?"

Joe motioned around him. "Here. In general. I know this isn't the most exciting life."

"I beg to differ," Tom replied with a naughty wink. "I'd say last night was pretty damn exciting. Good thing no one lives downstairs, or we might have had a few complaints about the noise."

Joe's face went up in flames, and he playfully kicked Tom under the table. "That's not what I meant. Also, I'm not the one with the dirty mouth." Thoughts of last night made Joe fidget in his seat. Tom had woken him up some time before dawn, ravishing Joe and driving him to the point of reckless abandonment. It was also when Joe discovered Tom's penchant for dirty talk.

Tom wriggled his eyebrows. "And I know what to do with it. Admit it, you love my dirty mouth."

"Oh for goodness sake. You're incorrigible." Joe was in serious danger of getting hard at the breakfast table. The man had no shame. He also wasn't wrong.

Tom chuckled and put his paper down. He leaned in, a wicked gleam in his eyes. "Can you blame me? The way you move is absolutely sinful, Mr. Applin. You keep that up and you'll never get rid of me."

Joe swallowed hard. *If only.* Joe had opened his mouth to reply when his cell phone buzzed. He checked it and sighed.

"The shop will be open in fifteen minutes. We should finish up. Thank you so much for making breakfast, and, um, for last night."

Tom finished his coffee and stood. He leaned in and gave Joe's cheek a kiss. "Believe me, it's my pleasure." He took Joe's earlobe between his teeth, sending a shiver through Joe. "I think I might be hooked on the taste of you, Joe. I hope you're prepared."

Joe didn't quite know what to do with himself. What would Bea do? Joe grimaced. It was far too early to be terrified. He turned his face and kissed Tom, surprising him. Tom was always the first to initiate an intimate moment. Maybe it was time for Joe to be a little bolder. He took hold of Tom's face and kissed him deeply, then slipped a hand under Tom's T-shirt to tweak a nipple, making Tom suck in a sharp breath.

"We'll see who's prepared," Joe murmured, nipping at Tom's stubbly jaw.

Tom groaned. "Looks like I'll be spending the day thinking of all the terrible things I'm going to do to you tonight."

"I'll be waiting," Joe purred, before getting up to clear the table. He'd never flirted so brazenly before. It felt… wonderful.

Joe was still a little worried Tom might get bored working the kitchen of the little café, but the man never complained and went about his duties with a smile. He looked happy. Joe hoped that by this point there was enough trust between them that Tom would confide in him if he wasn't happy.

Downstairs Tom helped Bea in the kitchen while Joe took the helm with Elsie at his side and Donnie took orders at the tables. The moment they opened the doors, they greeted the morning rush of customers in dire need of caffeine. Joe understood them perfectly. Nothing got done without a hefty dose of java. It was nonstop until after noon, when most folks were out to lunch. Many stopped by for some pie to take back to their offices or to save for later. The next rush would be in after most folks got off work. They'd drop by on their way home and pick up something for dessert, or they'd stop in for coffee with friends and to chat. The college kids and tourists were in at all hours. Once things slowed, Bea made Tom and Joe a small picnic and sent them into the garden for a while. Joe was on to her, but he wasn't about to tell her there had been more than pleasant conversation going on between them. Though judging by her smug grin when she saw them together, he'd hazard a guess that she already knew.

Joe was grateful for the little garden between his café and the boutique. He was the only one who seemed to use it, which suited him all the better. The small trees, shrubs, and potted plants made it all feel like some closed-off little corner of the world rather than a makeshift garden between two buildings in the middle of Manhattan. Their own little Central Park, without the traffic and tourists. They sat on the grass on a towel, their bellies full. They had a few more minutes before they had to go back to work.

"If I didn't know any better, I'd say Bea's playing matchmaker," Tom said with a smile.

"You'd be right. She's been trying to find me a man for years."

Tom cocked his head to one side, studying him curiously. "Surely it hasn't been that hard. A guy like you?"

Coming from anyone else, Joe would have thought he was being made fun of, but not from Tom. Tom appeared genuinely perplexed as to why Joe was still single. Had the guy not spent enough time in his company?

"Where do I start? I'm awkward, clumsy, talk to myself, sing to myself, argue with myself, wake up before the cows, believe you can taste memories, and I have nothing but this café. My only family is Bea, Donnie, and Elsie. I don't have many friends because I have trust issues, and I'm not exactly the most adventurous person."

Tom blinked at him. "I'm not sure I see the problem."

Joe let out a laugh. "Seriously? Believe me, it's sent more than one guy packing. That or the fact I never got past taking their number. Well, Bea would take their number. I'd say I'd call and then pretend I lost the number."

Tom wrapped his arm around Joe and pulled him in close, giving him a kiss. "Joe, everything you said makes you all the more endearing. Don't think of them as faults. Think of them as what makes you uniquely you. You're one of a kind. Any guy would be lucky to have you."

Joe worried his bottom lip with his teeth. Only one guy concerned him at the moment. Joe wanted to say so much to Tom. How happy he was that he was here, how the past few weeks had been amazing, how he wished Tom could stay…. Instead, he smiled at Tom and said, "Thank you."

Tom gave him another kiss before pushing himself to his feet. "Come on. We better head back in before Bea starts taking pictures."

Joe stared at him. "She's been watching us?"

"Yep. Like a hawk." Tom held his hand out, and Joe took it, allowing Tom to help him to his feet.

Joe shook his head. He wished he could say he was surprised, but he wasn't. She was probably dying to tell him she told him so. The woman was agile and crafty. She'd spring up from the darnedest places to tell him she was right, like some kind of white-haired ninja retiree.

Tom packed everything up, giving Joe one last kiss before he disappeared into the kitchen. Joe rolled his eyes as he passed Bea, who was grinning like the Cheshire Cat.

The rest of the day went off without a hitch. The shop was full, the customers were happy, and his little motley crew was all high-spirited, not that they didn't tend to be, but lately they seemed to be even more cheerful, and Joe wondered if something had been missing before that he hadn't been aware of. There certainly wasn't anything different about him, was there?

Soon it was closing time, and Joe bid farewell to the last customer. They all pitched in cleaning up, and Joe thanked everyone for another great day. He sent leftovers home with Donnie and Elsie, like he usually did. There was never a whole lot, but Joe would rather have leftovers at closing time than run out during the late-afternoon rush. It wasn't like he had trouble getting rid of it. Elsie's big brothers adored his pies and were always hopeful Elsie would be bringing some home. Donnie's dad was also a fan. The poor guy worked late at the docks, and Joe always made sure some pie was left for him. He was a good man and had raised Donnie on his own after Donnie's mom passed away when he was just a toddler.

Once everyone was gone, Joe turned to Tom. "How about I finish up and you use the shower? I'll be up in a minute."

Tom removed his apron and hung it up on the hook by the door. "You sure?"

"Positive. I won't be long."

"Okay. I'll get dinner started. How's pasta sound?" Tom's smile lit Joe up from the inside out.

"Sounds great." He enjoyed the view of Tom's gorgeous backside as he headed upstairs. Despite not being able to go to a gym, Tom had been able to keep himself in shape, exercising every morning and making do with whatever he had on hand, whether it was the stairs, bags of flour, sit-ups, pushups, lunges, or a host of other routines that exhausted Joe just by looking at it. Tom was convinced he'd get Joe to join him. Joe had a hearty laugh before stuffing his face full of cherry pie. His exercise came in the form of rushing around serving his customers, baking, and going up and down the stairs from his apartment to the shop.

Joe walked into the café and gave a start at finding a man standing there in a dark hoodie and jeans. How the heck had the guy gotten in? They'd locked all the doors.

"I'm sorry, but we're closed."

The front door opened and several more men stepped inside, all looking equally dangerous.

Joe tried not to panic, but it was hard. His mind raced, going back to that night when he'd been jumped and beaten. Had Blake sent them? Joe's heart leaped into his throat, and he took a step back. Not again. "We're closed, gentlemen. I'm afraid you have to leave."

One of the men in a leather jacket closed the door and locked it.

"Where is he?" Hoodie Guy hissed.

Behind him a man with a scar running down the side of his face joined him. "He asked you a question."

Joe carefully backed up toward the counter. "I don't know who you're talking about. Please leave before I call the police."

The men spread out across the shop. Hoodie Guy sneered. "Now that would be a very bad idea. I'm going to ask you again. Where is he?"

Joe swallowed hard. Who the hell were these guys? And why were they looking for Tom? Whatever they wanted from Tom, it couldn't be good. Maybe it was time to invest in a new alarm system. He hadn't updated the thing since it was installed years ago, and it had a habit of going on the fritz. Very little money was kept on-site, and he figured if someone was going risk stealing his ingredients or food processor, they might reconsider when they spotted the boutique next door that sold thousand-dollar shoes.

"Listen, I don't want any trouble," Joe said, hands up in front of him. What should he do? It was hard to concentrate when all he could think about was the men Blake's father had sent after him. His brow was beaded with sweat, and his hands felt clammy. *You need to do something, Joe. Don't just stand there waiting for them to hurt you. Do something!*

“Then tell us where he is,” Hoodie Guy growled. He nodded to one of his friends, who promptly grabbed an upturned chair off a table. Joe gave a terrible start and his pulse soared when the chair was bashed against the table several times before it splintered and broke into several pieces. The men grabbed several more chairs and broke them. They flipped over tables and knocked the framed pictures off the walls. They were tearing the place apart.

Hoodie made a grab for Joe, but Joe dove behind the counter. He snatched a hold of Bea’s baseball bat just as Hoodie guy raised his arms to grab Joe, leaving his ribs exposed, and giving Joe the perfect opportunity to whack him on the side with the bat. The guy doubled over in pain, and Joe slammed the bat down onto the man’s back before he kicked out, catching Hoodie guy in the face and bloodying his nose. The guy let out a barrage of curses as he pushed himself to his feet. Joe tried to get to his cell phone, but he was preoccupied swinging the baseball bat. He was about to yell for help when someone grabbed hold of the man’s hoodie and jerked him back, sending him skidding across the floor. Joe was frozen to the spot, gripping the bat against him, as Tom landed a fierce punch against one man’s face while he kicked out at another.

Joe wanted to help Tom, but he had the feeling he’d only end up getting in the way. He’d never seen anyone fight like that. Not outside the movies, anyway. It was like Tom knew what move his opponent was going to make before he made it. There was a fierceness in him Joe was seeing for the first time, yet he was calm, his moves calculated, like he’d done this plenty of times before. He grabbed one guy by the arm and flipped him over his back, then thrust his palm up against another guy's nose. One man against six, and Tom wasn't breaking a sweat.

One of the men pulled out a gun, and Joe cried out a warning. Tom snatched the man's gun and took it apart while the guy was still holding it. How had he done that? Tom was beating the pulp out of the men, and Joe wondered if he should call the police, but he had a feeling that would be a bad idea. Though how it could be worse than what was happening in his shop was beyond him, but how would they explain to the police about Tom, his amnesia, and his ability to leave six men writhing in pain? What if those detectives showed up again? Joe didn't trust them.

The men fell over each other, dripping blood and holding sore limbs as they tried to flee. Tom managed to grab hold of Hoodie Guy before he could make it to the door, but the guy unzipped his hoodie and fled.

"Dammit." Tom chucked the hoodie on the floor. Joe could tell he was tempted to go after them but decided against it. His chest rose and fell, but there was barely any sweat on his brow. He turned to Joe, his expression almost pained. "I should go."

"What?" Joe lowered the bat, taken aback when Tom walked into the garden. Joe followed, not quite ready to leave the bat behind. Tom paced. He stopped to look down at his knuckles, and that was when Joe saw the blood. Quickly, Joe went back in and picked up the small first aid kit from behind the counter, and went back out. Tom hadn't moved. He stood there staring down at his hands.

Joe removed an antiseptic wipe from its packet along with a roll of bandages. He stepped up to Tom and gently took his hands.

Tom flinched, as if he'd been in some kind of trance. When he spoke, his voice was hushed. "I'm so sorry, Joe."

"It's okay, Tom." Joe carefully wiped Tom's hands clean. They were still stained red, but Joe tenderly nursed them as best he could until the blood was gone, then wrapped the bandages around them. Tom's hands were steady, like nothing had happened.

"Okay? Those men were here for *me*. We both know that. They tore your shop apart. Did they hurt you?" Tom frantically checked him over. "Are you okay? Did they touch you? If they put their hands on you, so help me, I'll hunt them down and—"

"I'm fine. I promise."

Tom ran a hand through his hair, concern etched into his handsome face. "What if I hadn't arrived in time? What if one of those bastards had shot or stabbed you? I'd never forgive myself. Those men want me, not you. What if it had been Bea or Donnie or Elsie? I have to go. I can't put you in any more danger. If something happened to you because of me, I couldn't live with myself. These men mean serious business. They won't stop until they get their hands on me or someone ends up dead. I have to go."

"You can't be serious." Joe realized Tom wanted to protect him, but what difference would it make now? They believed Joe was involved, that he knew where Tom was. Yet the danger Joe was in would be nothing compared to what Tom might face out there on his own.

"Joe, listen to me." Tom put his hands on Joe's shoulders. "With every day that passes, the more danger I bring down on you and those around you. I should have left a long time ago."

"No."

Tom stared at him. "What?"

"I'm not letting you go out there on your own. Where are you going to go? You can't trust the police. You think I'm going to let you walk out into God knows what? Do you really think I'd just, what? Go about my business while you're hunted down? Go on as if nothing had happened, waiting for the day I hear about your death on the news?"

Tom frowned. "Thanks for the vote of confidence."

"You have skills, training—that much is obvious—but they have the advantage, Tom. You can't remember who you are. You don't know who these people are, why they want you, or what they'll do to you. There might be an entire army out there looking to get their hands on you, and you have no one on your side. As much as I'd like to boast about my batting skills, there's a reason I'm not playing for the Yankees." He needed to make Tom understand. "Going out there on your own without any information is suicide."

"Joe, be reasonable. Whoever these men are, they're willing to kill to get their hands on me." Tom shook his head. "My mind's made up. I'll find a shelter or somewhere to hide out until something comes back to me. Maybe I'll leave the state, head to Virginia." Tom went pensive. "There has to be a reason Virginia's the first state that popped into my head." He narrowed his eyes. "I have some kind of connection there."

Was Tom remembering? "What do you remember about Virginia?" Joe asked, hopeful.

"I… I don't know. It feels… important, though. It makes sense. I remember places. Colonial Williamsburg, Monticello, the caverns, Washington, DC. It's… so familiar. Yet here I am in New York City." Tom shook his head. "I should go."

"Don't leave me." Joe was caught off guard by his words. He hadn't expected them to come out. They'd been swimming around in his head for some time, and now seemed as good a time as any to let them out. He'd done it. He'd asked Tom to stay. Joe worried his bottom lip with his teeth before speaking up again, his brows drawn together. His voice was so quiet, he wondered if Tom had heard him at all considering he hadn't said a word.

"Please." Joe took a step toward him. "We'll figure something out together, but don't go. Not now, not after…."

Tom swallowed hard. "What are you trying to tell me, Joe? After what?"

"I just… I don't want to lose you. I know we're dealing with a lot of uncertainty here, and there's a good chance I might end up losing you anyway, when you remember, but until then… I'd like you to stay with me. I kinda got used to having you around." Joe tried not to fidget. His face was flushed, and he was having trouble meeting Tom's gaze. Joe cared about him, wanted him to stay here with him.

"How long have you been worrying I'd leave after regaining my memory?" Tom asked gently.

"A while," Joe admitted. "I know I'm being selfish. Whoever you are, your life's clearly more exhilarating. The places you've been to, the way you handle yourself, the shape you're in." Joe let out a sigh. "You shouldn't be cooped up here."

Tom drew Joe into his arms. "Even a wandering man yearns for a home to go back to, Joe. It's true, I'm not so good at being still for long, but that doesn't mean I don't want to be here. I like being around too. I'll stay. God knows I want to. We'll have to be more careful. I don't want you getting hurt. I need to think about my next course of action. Whoever those men were, they'll be back. You, Bea, Donnie, Elsie, and the customers who come in here every day need to be kept safe. I can't put them at risk again. What if these men return during the day? The public has to be protected from men like those, from men who swore an oath only to spit on the promise they'd made." There was no mistaking the conviction in Tom's voice.

"You feel strongly about that, don't you?"

"I do." Tom's expression hardened. "I won't let those lowlifes or the men they work for hurt innocent people. They don't care who gets hurt in their quest for greed and power." Tom pulled away and closed his eyes, his brows drawn together.

"Tom? What's wrong?"

"There's something there. I can almost see it." He opened his eyes and looked around. "This garden. I came here for a reason. I was running from them. I knew to come here." He slowly walked around the garden, taking in everything around him. "Why would I come here? If I was running from them, why would I pick this spot?"

Tom concentrated and followed whatever train of thought he was on. Had Tom really come *here* specifically? Why? Joe had never seen him before that night, so why would Tom choose this garden? Tom stopped again and closed his eyes. He breathed in deeply and let it out slowly through his mouth.

"Coming in here would mean jumping the fence. If I was in danger, being chased, why take the chance of getting cornered?" He opened his eyes again and crouched down. Joe followed his lead, crouching down beside him.

"There's nothing here but grass, dirt, and potted flowers," Joe muttered. If there had been anything here, Joe would have found it the night he found Tom. It wasn't the first time they'd checked the garden. Tom had been out here plenty of times, hoping it would jog his memory, but nothing ever came to him, until now.

Tom cocked his head to one side. "Dirt and flowers. There were dirt and flower petals in my pocket when you found me." He picked up a pot of pink geraniums. "Pink petals."

"These are the only pink flowers out here," Joe pointed out. "Look." He placed his finger to one flower in the bunch. "This one's missing some petals."

"So, how'd they get in my pocket?" Tom asked.

"You think you plucked them and put them in your pocket? That doesn't make any sense."

Tom sighed. "None of this makes sense." He studied the flowers and fingered the dirt, a frown coming onto his face. He stood and walked over to one of the light fixtures. "There are indentations in the dirt." He dug through the soil, his eyes widening. "There's something in here." Tom dug in and pulled something out.

"What is it?" Joe asked him. All he could see between Tom's fingers was a small lump of dirt.

Tom handed Joe the flowerpot and wiped what he'd found with the end of his T-shirt. He held it up to the light. It was a tiny black plastic case.

Joe peered at it. "Looks like one of those SD cards you store pictures on."

"Among other things," Tom replied. "Joe, I need to use your laptop."

Joe gave him a nod. He returned the potted plant to where they'd found it and quickly went inside, with Tom insisting on going ahead and checking the place out first. He made sure all the windows and doors were secure before they headed upstairs to Joe's apartment. Tom said he'd wait in the kitchen while Joe grabbed his laptop from the bedroom. As he did, he wondered if Tom buried that SD card in the pot of geraniums. It had to be. It would explain why Joe had found Tom in the garden and why there had been dirt and petals in his pocket. Had Tom put them in there as a clue to himself? Why else would they be in his pocket?

It was like some kind of spy movie or something. Joe had to admit he was intrigued, and a little excited. He met Tom in the kitchen at the breakfast nook, where Tom sat. Joe placed the laptop in front of him and booted it up, thanking Tom when he slid over so Joe could sit beside him. Joe was dying to find out what was going on almost as much as Tom. Maybe this was it. Maybe whatever was on that card could help them identify Tom.

The moment the laptop booted up, Tom slipped the SD card in. A black screen appeared prompting for a password. Dammit. For a second Joe thought they'd been on to something. Whatever it was, Tom hid it in that plant.

"It's encrypted." Tom studied the screen and the blinking cursor.

"Well, so much for that," Joe muttered. At least that's what Joe thought until Tom started typing away. A second black screen popped up with scrolling white text before a spreadsheet opened.

Joe's jaw dropped. "How did you do that?"

Tom stared at the screen. "I don't know. I just… did it. I put my fingers to the keyboard and went with my gut. This all seems familiar. Bypassing the encryption, I mean. I have no idea what this list is. I feel like I should know, like it's the key to everything."

They studied the sheet. There were several columns. The first contained names, the second random numbers, the third large sums that appeared to be dollars and cents, and the final column contained dates. The bottom of the spreadsheet had tabs separated by months.

"Hold on." Tom perked up. "If I check the file's info, I might be able to see who the creator was."

"Great idea!" If Tom knew how to get past the encryption, there was a chance he might be the file's creator. When the window popped up, they stared at it as if it held the secrets to the universe. They were disappointed to find merely a set of initials.

"LB." Tom pressed his lips together before letting out a sigh. "I don't know what that means."

"Could they be your initials?" Joe asked hopefully.

"Maybe, but that doesn't help much. They could stand for anything." Tom returned to the spreadsheet. "This looks like some kind of bookkeeping software." Tom clicked on something else and another folder popped up. This one contained receipts, invoices, and bills. Another folder was filled with images.

"These look like surveillance photos."

Joe glanced at Tom. "How do you know?"

"Look at the time stamps. Then there's the angles and the distance. It's obvious whoever took them was trying to stay out of sight. Also, none of the men in this picture seem to be aware they're being photographed. Bookkeeping software, surveillance photos, paperwork. Someone's been gathering intel on these guys."

Joe glimpsed at the spreadsheet and froze. "Wait a second. There." He pointed to the screen, a chill going up his spine. "Romero and McCrea. Those were the names of the detectives who came looking for you a few weeks back."

"These names all look familiar."

"Well, we know two of them are detectives." Whatever this list was, it couldn't be on the up and up. He was right not to trust those two.

Joe opened the web browser and typed one of the names from the list into the search. It came back with hundreds of hits. They stared at the screen.

"That guy's a judge." Joe couldn't believe it. Was this….

"If I'm not mistaken," Tom said gravely, "I think this is a list of people on the take, and I'm willing to bet the men in these pictures are on this list."

Before Joe could ask why Tom would have all this, the buzzer rang. Tom swiftly removed the SD card and shut the laptop. He placed the card in the case, and Joe took it from him.

"What are you doing?" Tom asked him.

"It's a safe bet that whoever's after you is after this. It's better if I hold on to it until we can get it to the proper authorities. I don't know who that is yet, but we'll figure it out." The buzzer rang again, and Tom slid out of the booth. Joe followed. He headed toward the door that led downstairs.

"Joe, I think you should stay up here," Tom advised him.

"The last guys didn't knock. They broke in. If I don't answer, it'll look suspicious. I'm going to check who it is. It might be the cops. Someone might have heard the disturbance and called them."

"And if they're on that list?" Tom asked, following Joe downstairs.

"Then I don't know, but you need to stay out of sight."

Tom grabbed Joe's arm before he could reach the bottom step. "I'm not leaving you to face who knows what alone."

"Just stay here. If I need you to go all Jason Bourne on their asses, I'll shout."

Tom didn't look convinced. "Okay, fine. But be careful. I'll be waiting."

Joe gave Tom a quick kiss before walking out into the kitchen and then through the doors into the café. The place looked like a warzone. Taking a deep breath, Joe approached the front door and prayed whoever was on the other side was someone they could trust.

Chapter Nine

"**MR.** Applin?"

Joe cautiously opened the door, relieved when no one tried to kick it in. Instead, he saw two men in dark suits and a huge black Suburban parked out front. "Yes?"

"We're with the Federal Bureau of Investigation. May we have a word with you?"

The FBI? Was that a good thing or a bad thing? Had there been any agents on that list of Tom's? Not like they would know. It wasn't like bureau agents went around with name badges. These guys only showed up when there was real trouble, and most of the time they did so under the radar. "Could I see your identification? You can't be too careful these days."

"Certainly." The taller of the men pulled out a black wallet and flipped it open. "I'm Agent Baker, this is Agent Johnson."

Why were agents always called Johnson? Joe opened the door and let the men inside. "What can I do for you, gentlemen?"

"We have reason to believe you may be in danger." Agent Baker looked around the café with a frown. "Is everything okay, Mr. Applin?"

"Yeah, um, we had a break-in. I was out getting some groceries. They must have run off when they realized there was nothing to steal. Unless flour has suddenly become priceless, there's nothing of value here."

"Have you called the police?" Agent Johnson asked, his expression unreadable. The man looked like he was carved from stone.

"Not yet. I just got home." Joe rubbed his arm and looked around. "I'm still a little shaken up about it."

"It's possible this wasn't your typical break-in," Agent Baker said. "We've been hunting a suspect who we believe is working for one of the local drug cartels as a hired gunman. He's exceptionally skilled and extremely lethal. Our sources tell us he may have stolen something from his bosses, and now they're after him. We'd like to get to him first."

"And you think he's close by?" Joe asked innocently.

Agent Baker cocked his head to one side as he studied Joe. "Mr. Applin, you seem like a good man. Hardworking, just trying to make a living. This lowlife preys on good people like you. Manipulates them, uses lies to get them to help him, to hide him. Then, when he has no more use for them, he gets rid of them. This guy has local authorities after him, the federal government, criminal organizations, and it's only a matter of time before he brings it all down on whoever's helping him."

Joe stared at them. "And you think *I'm* helping him?" He let out a small laugh. "I bake pies. The most excitement I see around here is the morning rush for extra-strong coffee." He motioned around him. "This isn't a typical day for me, Agent Baker." Baker…. "Agent Baker, were you ever an officer for the NYPD?"

"No, sir. Chicago. It's a common surname."

"Oh. Right." It was a shot in the dark. He thought maybe there was a chance it had been the man who saved him, but Joe would have thought he'd feel something familiar if it had been.

Agent Johnson pointed toward the end of the café. "Would you mind if we took a look around?"

"No, of course not. I'll turn on the lights to the rest of the shop so you can get a better look at everything." He motioned around him. "Help yourself. I can make you some coffee in the meantime."

"No, thank you. We won't be here long."

Joe gave them a nod and casually headed to the back just as Tom came down the stairs. Joe rushed over.

"Joe?"

"The FBI is here." His heart was pounding fiercely, and his hands were shaking. These weren't just some hoodlums. How the hell were they supposed to face the FBI?

"What?"

"They're saying you're a gun for hire. That you worked for a drug cartel and now you're on the run because you stole something from them." So much of what the agents said made sense, and what reason did they have to lie? And yet….

Tom shook his head. "That can't be true." He looked uncertain, and Joe hated that he felt a little scared. If Tom wasn't who they said he was, he would have been sure, wouldn't he? He would have denied it, felt it deep in his gut. Joe was terrified by the fear in Tom's eyes.

"Tom?"

"I.... No, it can't be." Tom gently cupped Joe's face. How could those be the eyes of a cold-blooded killer? "I'm not a murderer. I know it's my word against theirs, but you have to believe me. Joe, you know me." He placed Joe's hand against his chest over his heart. "In here. You know I'm not a killer."

Joe leaned in and kissed Tom. It was quick but deep and filled with as much passion as Joe possessed. "I'm sorry, Tom." He pulled Tom against him and whispered in his ear, "The garden. Run."

Tom looked up past Joe to the kitchen, his eyes going wide. Joe spun around and bolted, slamming through the swinging kitchen doors and into the two agents. The three of them went tumbling through, landing on the floor in the café. Joe scrambled to his feet, stunned to find Tom still standing in the kitchen.

"Run!"

Tom snapped out of it and took off toward the side exit. Joe ran out the front door of the shop, crying out when several men grabbed Tom the moment he landed on the other side of the fence. *No!* They'd been waiting for him.

Joe made to go after Tom, to do something to help him, but he was apprehended by Agent Baker. "Please don't hurt him! I know you think he's a killer, but he's not," Joe begged the agent holding him, his heart splintering as Tom struggled against his captors.

"Joe!" Tom slammed his shoulder into one of the men holding him and broke into a run, but he didn't get very far before he was tackled to the ground. He hit the cement with a thud, and Joe flinched at the obvious pain it caused him. Despite the men struggling to detain him, Tom was more concerned about Joe than his own dire predicament.

"Let go of him, you son of a bitch!" Joe said.

They dragged Tom to his feet, and he fought fiercely as he tried to reach for Joe. Their fingers brushed against each other's, and Joe's eyes filled with tears.

"You've got the wrong man! He's not a killer. I know he isn't!"

"Joe, you can't—" A blow to his stomach cut Tom off, and he doubled over with a growl. Oh God, what were they going to do to him?

Agent Baker shook his head. "You're a good man, Mr. Applin. He's trying to get your sympathy. That's what he does. Prey on the kindhearted."

"He's not a killer!" Joe spat out. "You don't know him like I do! Please, can we talk about this?" His heart was torn to shreds as Tom struggled against the agents. Every time Tom screamed his name, another piece of Joe's heart was ripped from his chest and his eyes burned from the tears he held back. Did they have to be so rough?

"Agent Baker, please." Joe grabbed the man's wrist when Tom stopped fighting, his eyes wide as he looked from Joe to Agent Baker. Something in Tom's face, in his eyes, the way he stared at the other man made Joe still. Then he heard it.

"Joe, that's not Agent Baker! He's—" Tom's words died on his lips as the group of agents threw a black bag over his head and hauled him off his feet, rushing him to the backseat of a black Suburban that pulled up to the curb.

They were taking him away. What if Joe never saw him again? It couldn't end this way. They were wrong. Tom wasn't a killer.

The cocking of a gun snapped Joe out of his trance, and someone kicked the back of his legs, forcing him onto his knees. What the hell was going on? The world seemed to slow as Agent Baker aimed a gun at him. A shot rang out and Joe flinched. Tom screamed his name, and a car door slammed. Tires skidded and more tires screeched to a halt. Joe's pulse was racing. Had he been shot? He looked down at himself, feeling his chest. He was so confused.

"I'm okay," Joe said, his voice almost a whisper. He looked down at the man writhing in pain on the sidewalk, a puddle of blood forming under him.

Half a dozen men in suits came running, and two of them took away the man on the ground. A tall fair-haired man flashed a badge at Joe.

"I'm Agent Geoffrey, FBI. Mr. Applin, I need you to come with me. We'll talk on pursuit."

"Pursuit?" Joe grew more confused by the moment. Another agent handed a wallet to Agent Geoffrey, who flipped it open and nodded. "I don't understand. Why was Agent Baker going to shoot me? And why did you shoot him? Isn't he one of yours?"

"I'll explain in the car. Trust me."

Joe pushed himself to his feet. "To be honest, I don't know who to trust anymore."

Agent Geoffrey met his gaze as he helped him up. "Mr. Applin, if you want to save your friend, you'll come with me right now."

What choice did he have? Joe quickly climbed into the back of a large black Suburban. The tires screeched as they took off, sirens blaring and lights flashing. Joe swiftly buckled up. At this time of night there wasn't as much traffic, but it was still busy. Joe held on to the door for dear life as the line of black vehicles sped north through the city, running red lights and avoiding other cars, along with pedestrians. He sure hoped they didn't get killed on the way to save Tom. Speaking of *they*….

"All right, Agent Geoffrey, what the hell's going on? Why did those men take Tom?"

"Mr. Applin. That man we shot was not Agent Baker. The real Agent Baker is the man who was just kidnapped. The man you've been calling Tom. It's likely the men looking for Liam suspected he was hiding at your shop and were attempting to draw him out by using his name."

"What?" Had he heard right? No, it wasn't possible.

"Tom's real name is Liam Baker, and he's a federal agent. We've been searching for him for weeks." Agent Geoffrey let out a deep breath. "You did one hell of a job hiding him. Though we still don't know why he didn't make contact, or why he chose you."

"Oh my God," Joe gasped.

"Don't worry," Agent Geoffrey assured him. "Liam will buy us some time until we get there."

"Liam? Oh, right." *His name is Liam….*

"He's been in tough spots before."

Joe ran his fingers through his hair and shook his head. "What if he can't buy himself time? What if we get there too late and they kill him?" This was so much worse than he thought.

"Really, Mr. Applin. Liam's highly experienced."

Joe shook his head. "Liam might be, but what about Tom?"

"I don't follow." Agent Geoffrey tapped at his earpiece, speaking to someone on the other end. It looked like they were heading up Henry Hudson Parkway. Didn't they understand? Didn't they *know*?

"The reason Tom—I mean, Liam—didn't get into contact with you is because he lost his memory." It was all falling into place. His training, his skills, the precision with which he did things, the way he retained information down to the tiniest details, the events leading up to Joe finding him. At least from what Joe could piece together.

"Come again?"

Yeah, it sounded crazy even to him, and he knew it to be the truth. "When I found him, he couldn't remember who he was. Not even his name. What if he can't remember his training?"

Agent Geoffrey was stunned. "Are you telling me Liam has *amnesia*?"

"I know how it sounds, believe me, but it's true. I found him in the garden next to my shop. He was bleeding from a blow to the back of the head, but he refused to go to the hospital, begged me to help him, and wouldn't let me call the cops. Kept saying he'd end up dead."

"That's because Liam was working undercover, posing as a hired gunman for a local drug cartel. We've been after them for months, but every time we received information on a shipment, we'd find nothing. Someone was tipping them off. They were always a step ahead. Liam was familiar with the territory. So he was sent undercover. The last message we received said he had what we needed, but somewhere en route to drop off the package, he disappeared, fell completely off the grid. We worried he may have been made."

"McCrea and Romero."

"I'm sorry?"

"Two detectives who came into the shop looking for Tom. I got a bad feeling about them, so I lied. Told them I hadn't seen the man they were looking for." Joe slipped his hand into his pocket and pulled out the SD card. He handed it to Agent Geoffrey. "Their names are on this list."

Agent Geoffrey took the card from him, his eyes wide. "Where did you get this?"

"Tom—I mean Liam—found it buried in the garden in a potted plant. We think he stashed it there before he was assaulted. It would explain why there was nothing but dirt and flower petals in his pockets when I found him. It's encrypted, but he knew what to do. He was able to access it. It has a long list of names, numbers, and figures, surveillance photos, invoices, and a bunch of other stuff. Those detectives were on the list, along with a court judge."

"That's what Liam found. Dirty officials on the cartel's payroll. No wonder we kept hitting a wall. Damn it. Someone on that list must have made Liam."

Joe grabbed a hold of Geoffrey's arm. "When they find out he doesn't have it…."

Agent Geoffrey tapped his earpiece. "We need to catch these guys, *now*."

Joe looked out his window. Up ahead he could see the exit for Inwood Hill Park. Jesus, they were going to drag Tom into the dark woods. How the hell were they supposed to find him in all those dense trees? The closer they got to the place, the more anxious Joe became. He tried not to think of the poor innocent people who'd been found dead in that park over the years. He dug his fingers into the passenger side door. If anyone could save Tom, it was the FBI, right? They had to be as experienced as Tom. Liam. Dammit. He had to get used to that.

The sirens blared and lights flashed as they sped down the parkway in a convoy of huge black vehicles. Joe had no idea if the men who took Liam were still ahead of them or already in the park. Within minutes, their vehicle came to a stop outside the park. Everyone jumped to action, and Joe silently slid out, aware of the resonating sound of cocking firearms. Agent Geoffrey rounded everyone up and gave instructions.

"Spread out. I want Agent Baker returned alive."

Alive? Oh God. The gravity of the situation hit Joe hard. What if the men killed Liam? There was so much Joe wanted to say to him. They were so close to the truth. Did Liam remember who he was? Joe stood by, feeling useless, but what could he do? These were professionals. This was what they did. Agent Geoffrey spotted him and hurried over.

"Stay here, Mr. Applin."

Joe nodded as dozens of agents disappeared into the darkened forest. All Joe could think about was Liam, in there somewhere, against who knew what, in danger.

Please, be okay. You have to be okay.

LIAM remembered everything.

He remembered hitting his head on the radiator when he was a kid after not listening to his mom about jumping on the bed. He had to get stitches and to this day had a faint scar on his left eyebrow. Then there was the time he'd chased his sister into the basement of their neighbor's house while their mom got a perm and he scraped his head on the unpolished banister. He bled but thankfully no stitches were needed. He really needed to stop hitting his head. Everything was there, everything before today, including the first time he saw Joe's deep blue-green eyes.

There was no way in hell he wasn't making it out of this. Joe was alive. For a moment he'd been terrified, thinking that son of a bitch imposter had shot Joe, but when he heard the sirens, heard the bastards arguing about leaving the "pie guy" behind, he knew Joe was safe. Geoffrey had found him. Liam could always count on his partner to come through for him.

They'd been walking for miles. During that time, Liam had been studying his captors and his surroundings. The men stopped in a clearing. Someone jerked him to a halt before kicking at the back of Liam's knees and forcing him down onto the dirt, his hands zip-tied in front of him. All he needed was the right opportunity, but first he needed to buy himself some time. His team wouldn't be far. He'd be surprised if they weren't already tracking him.

"Where is it?" one guy growled.

"Where's what?" Liam asked, adding a slight tremor to his voice.

A punch snapped Liam's head to one side, splitting his lip and leaving a slight copper taste in his mouth. He remembered the taste well, along with the blood, broken bones, bruises, and everything else that came with being a field agent. He remembered being shot at, punched, grazed by a runaway truck, and a host of other injuries he'd acquired while taking down drug-peddling assholes like these.

"Where's the package?"

Liam spit out saliva tinged with blood. "I don't know what you're talking about."

One of the dark-haired goons holding a rifle sneered. "Don't play dumb with us. We know you're a Fed. Matteo wants your head for your betrayal."

Matteo would want someone's head for sneezing. The guy was a hotheaded nasty piece of work, ruthless in his quest to expand his empire. He started out small, taking over his father's drug running business before the shipments went from drugs, to firearms, and finally people. It had taken a hell of a lot of restraint on Liam's part to act indifferent to the freighter hauling young men and women, some of them underage and others barely legal. All to be sold or forced into prostitution. That's when Liam swore to himself that he'd do whatever it took to take down Matteo and the filth who worked for him. "I don't know what or who you're talking about. Look, I don't remember anything. All I know is someone assaulted me. Hit me in the back of the head hard. When I woke up, I couldn't remember my own name. Whoever you think I am, whatever you believe I have, I don't remember."

The half-dozen armed men exchanged glances before bursting into laughter.

"You expect us to believe that?" one of them chimed in.

"Check this guy out. I didn't know Feds had a sense of humor."

Liam shook his head. "Do you really think if I was who you say I am that I wouldn't have run off to the cops? That I wouldn't have done whatever I was supposed to do with this package you're after? You've been after me for how long? I've been washing dishes and baking pies, man. Does that sound like something a Fed would do while he's being chased by God knows who?"

The men seemed to think on that.

One of the guys frowned. "He's got a point, Castro. Dude's been hanging out in a pie shop."

"Bullshit. If that was true, then how come he kicked the shit out of Santo and his guys? This guy wiped the floor with them." The head moron in charge marched up to Liam and smacked him with the butt of his machine gun. Stars appeared in the front of Liam's eyes, and he sucked in a sharp breath. His face was in serious pain, but he couldn't make a move. Not yet. Before he could recover, he was punched across the face and kicked in the chest. He wheezed and drew in a lungful of air as he fell onto his side. He was kicked a couple more times for good measure, pain shooting through his body. Liam tightened his abs and covered his head as best he could with his restrained hands.

"We need him alive, you idiot," another gunman hissed.

The guy who'd kicked him jerked him back onto his knees in front of him. "If you can't *remember*, maybe we'll go back and ask your boyfriend." He laughed as he squeezed Liam's cheeks.

The hell you will. Liam murmured something under his breath.

"What was that?" The guy leaned in closer. "I can't hear you."

"I said," Liam ground out through gritted teeth, "I'd like to see you try." He made fists and thrust his elbows back with all his strength just as he smacked his head forward, head-butting the guy as he snapped the zip tie restraining him. Liam threw a hand out and grabbed hold of the guy's shirt, snatching the machine gun away with his other hand. Knowing what came next, Liam spun the guy in front of him, using him as a shield. He could almost kiss the guy for wearing a vest. Instead, he fired at the guy's associates as he backed up toward some trees. No honor among thieves. They fired at him, hitting their friend wherever they could in the hopes of getting Liam.

When Liam was in the clear, he released his screaming and bloodied friend and took off into the woods. The men shot as they chased after him into the darkened mass of trees. Liam knew the place well. He'd come here plenty of times with his parents when he was a kid and then with friends when he was older. If he kept down this path, he'd end up on Payson Avenue a few yards from the playground. Liam fired behind him at no one in particular. All he had to do was continue making enough noise and his team would find him. They'd close in on the bastards and take them down.

Liam ducked and dodged, running around trees, and over boulders and fallen trees. The shooting continued and a bullet grazed Liam's arm.

"Shit." He ducked behind a tree. In the distance he could hear shouting and see the faint glow of flashlights. His captors were closing in on him. If he called out now, he'd give away his position. Forget waiting for backup. It was time to take matters into his own hands. Liam checked the magazine of the machine gun. He was tired of being hunted. It was time to become the hunter.

Liam slipped into a thicket of trees and crouched down in the shadows. He grabbed a rock and tossed it far across to the other side, where it hit a tree. Two of the men rushed forward, their guns ready. Liam fired twice, one bullet per guy, catching them both in the legs. They dropped to the ground, shooting blindly as they screamed and writhed in pain. Three down. Three more to go. Liam silently and swiftly left his hiding spot to duck behind a large tree. He peeked out, grinning. The three men were out in the open, exposed. Liam's adrenaline was pumping. He smiled to himself. It was good to be back.

A SERIES of shots rang out somewhere close-by, and Joe gave a start. "Oh no." It was Liam, he just knew it. Joe took off, ignoring the shouts of the men who'd stayed behind with him. He had to go to Liam, make sure he was all right. Joe sped off in the direction the sound had come from. There he was putting his safety at risk, but he couldn't think about anything except Liam. It was strange thinking of Tom as Liam. Whatever name he used, it wouldn't change what had happened over the last few weeks. It wouldn't change how Joe felt.

Running through the woods, Joe was aware of the dozens of agents running along with him, guns in hand. Joe prayed Liam was safe and that he was able to call on his training as he had in the shop. Liam could handle himself; Joe had to trust in him. Maybe he even remembered who he was. All this had to jog some kind of instinct or reaction, some memory recall.

In the distance he spotted a man holding a gun standing over an injured man, and Joe's heart almost stopped, until he realized the man holding the gun was Liam. Joe came to a halt when he reached him, stunned to find three men scattered around on the ground writhing in pain. Liam had done this on his own?

The Feds closed in, rushing the men and detaining them. One officer arrived to take the machine gun from Liam. When Liam spotted Joe, he hurried over and pulled Joe into his arms.

"Thank God you're all right. I was so worried."

"*You* were worried?" Joe pulled away. "When they took you, I was terrified." He noticed the blood on Liam's arm. "You're bleeding!"

Liam released him, seeming to remember they weren't alone, especially as an EMT was heading their way. "It's just a graze. Thank you for coming."

"Of course I came. I was so afraid they'd hurt you." Joe swallowed hard as they escorted the men away, cursing and shouting. Joe had witnessed arrests before, but never anything like this. Liam pulled Joe to one side, his expression troubled.

"I'm okay, Joe. How about you? Are you all right?"

Not remotely, but he nodded anyway. The EMT spoke to Liam, asking him questions before she got to work on his arm. "So this is what you do." Joe glanced over at one of the gunman being taken away.

"Sometimes. Other times it's a lot of sitting around waiting, filling out paperwork."

Joe turned his attention back to Liam. "You're a G-Man."

Liam chuckled. A mischievous gleam came into his eyes. "Guess it's better than a nutritionist."

Joe arched an eyebrow at him. "Not funny." Liam laughed, and Joe shoved his hands into his pockets, aware of the chaotic scene going on around them as agents dealt with the crime scene. He waited for the EMT to finish up with Liam, and once she'd walked away, he spoke up. "So, what happens now?"

"First things first." Liam held his hand out with a smile. "Liam Baker, FBI."

Joe took his hand with a sad smile. "Nice to meet you, Liam."

Someone called out Liam's name, and Joe's heart sank a little. "You should get going. They probably have a lot of questions for you. I gave the SD card to Agent Geoffrey."

"He's my partner at the bureau, and a good guy." Liam's expression softened, and he placed his hand on the small of Joe's back, leading him back in the direction of the parked government vehicles. "I need to take care of this, but as soon as I'm done, I'll come by the café. We need to talk. I'll send people over to clean up and get you some new chairs."

"That's not necessary," Joe assured him.

"No, it is. Please."

Joe nodded and did his best to smile, but his heart was breaking. This was it. This was what he'd feared. He couldn't blame Tom—Liam. The man had a life, one he'd lived just fine before meeting Joe. He had a career and maybe someone special back home. Even if he didn't have someone, Liam was a federal agent. What would he want with a man who baked pies for a living? Joe was happy with what he did. He loved what he did, but he could understand how that might not be the most exciting lifestyle for a man of action like Liam.

The ride back was quiet. Agent Geoffrey took Joe's statement, recording the conversation as Joe explained everything he believed was relevant to their case from the moment he'd found Liam until the FBI showed up. Of course he left out personal details, like their nights in front of the TV together, enjoying each other's company, or the way Liam had made him feel like he was the most desired man in the world. Their intimate moments, caresses, embraces, the way Liam drove him crazy with his kisses, or the way Liam brought him to his knees. Their nights making love, teasing each other. Joe didn't bring up any of that. He didn't mention how much he missed Liam already.

Joe wished Liam had been able to ride with him, but their supervisor wanted to hear from Liam right away regarding his disappearance and any information he might have on the men they arrested. Liam was reluctant to leave him, but Joe assured him he'd be fine.

They dropped Joe off at the café after insisting he call the number on the card he was given if he thought of anything else or needed anything at all. Joe stood in the middle of his little shop, splintered chairs and upturned tables all around. Broken glass on the floor from the picture frames. He just didn't have the energy to do anything about it tonight. He turned off the lights and went upstairs, showered, and got into bed. He would have thought maybe he'd return home to police cars and questioning, but there was no one. It was as if nothing happened.

Joe lay in his big bed all alone and stared at his ceiling. It was so quiet. Liam was probably still up debriefing. What would he tell his superiors about the time he'd spent here? Joe rolled onto his side, his heart aching. Liam was from a completely different world. He spent his time chasing down criminals, investigating, traveling all over the country. He'd never be happy here with Joe, in his tiny little apartment above a pie shop.

That night Joe barely slept. He'd tossed and turned, trying to come to grips with everything that had happened. The next morning when he came downstairs, he thought he must still be dreaming. The place was spotless. Everything had been swept, cleaned up, fixed, replaced, and gleamed good as new. Joe had to admit, he was impressed. Having a G-Man for a boyfriend might have some perks. *If only.* Joe spent the rest of the morning assuring Bea, Donnie, and Elsie that he was all right.

"Wow, I can't believe Tom—I mean, Liam—is a Fed! How cool is that!" Donnie was still in awe, had been since Joe had told them what happened last night. Of course he left out all the shooting. They'd fuss over him, and he didn't want them worrying. At least they were safe now.

"I knew that boy was a hero," Bea proclaimed, and Joe almost spit out his coffee.

"You thought he was an assassin sent to bump me off!"

Bea waved a hand in dismissal. "I think the excitement has gotten to you."

The bell above the shop door jingled. Joe turned to greet his customer and his stomach filled with butterflies. Liam stood there, dressed in a charcoal-gray suit, white button-down shirt, and a black tie. He looked more handsome than ever. It took Joe a second to snap himself out of it.

"Look at you, all respectable," Joe teased. He reached out to straighten Liam's collar, though there wasn't really anything to straighten out. It was silly, to have missed the man so terribly after one night. "You look good."

"Thanks," Liam replied with a shy smile. He motioned to one of the empty booths near the back of the café, and Joe followed him, taking a seat across from him. "I was on my way to the New York office and wanted to stop by to say thank you for everything you've done for me. Because of you, we're moving in on the cartel and everyone on their payroll."

"Me?" Joe shook his head. "That was all you. You put your life on the line to get that intel. You were almost killed."

"If you hadn't taken me in, put your faith in a man you didn't even know, I would have been. Those detectives who came by looking for me were working for the cartel. I've been collecting intel on those men for months, hoping they would lead me to more dirty officials. They were the ones who made me, and spread the word after I took off. If you'd trusted them, handed me over, they would have killed me, or one of their corrupt buddies would have. So, thank you." Liam placed his hand over Joe's. "There's so much I want to say, Joe, but I have some things I need to do first. The government waits for no man. I'll come by as soon as I can. I promise."

"I understand." Joe meant it. He had no idea how these things worked, but he knew enough to know what Liam and his team had accomplished, what they were in the middle of, was no small feat, and the aftermath would keep them busy for some time. As much as it broke Joe's heart, he'd known this day would come. Even so, he wasn't prepared. All he could do was his best, try and be brave.

"Joe." Liam squeezed his hand. "I *will* be back. I promise. I'm not walking away from us."

Joe blinked at him. "Us?"

The bell jingled and a familiar voice called Joe's name, making him flinch. Dammit, of all the rotten timing. Did the guy not have anything better to do than harass him? Blake appeared beside their table, his upturned lip aimed at them. He looked Liam over with obvious disdain.

"What the hell are you doing here?" Joe asked, unable to believe the guy had come back.

"I've come to give you a second chance. Cater my event and I won't press charges against you and your guard dog."

Joe stood to face Blake. He was done shrinking away from his past. Blake had taken enough away from him. Joe wasn't about to go down without a fight, not this time. "Get the hell out."

Blake shoved his hands into his pockets and took a look around the café. "You know, it would be a shame if a city inspector came and found this place infested with roaches. He'd have to shut you down."

"What?" Did the guy have no shame? Why wasn't he surprised Blake would sink so low?

Blake's toothy grin made Joe want to punch him. "You know better than to cross me, Joe. Just give me what I want and everyone walks away happy."

Before Joe could tell him what he could do with his threat, Liam was on his feet, looking imposing and dangerous. Should Joe feel guilty Blake recoiled at Liam's presence? Who was he kidding? Blake deserved whatever Liam gave him.

Liam rounded his shoulders, his expansive chest as impressive as his menacing scowl. "Leave right now, or I'll have you arrested for conspiracy to bribe a public official."

Blake laughed. "You think because you put on a cheap suit, the police are going to believe *you*?"

"Oh, I think they might." Liam smiled pleasantly and reached into the inside pocket of his suit jacket. He flipped open a wallet and presented his badge. "I don't believe we've been properly introduced. Agent Liam Baker. FBI."

Blake's jaw nearly became unhinged. He stared at the badge before moving his gaze to Liam. "That has to be fake."

Liam shrugged. "Maybe. And maybe after I arrest you, the federal government will take a nice long look at your finances, and your dad's. Go over everything with a fine-tooth comb. We'll look into every account, IRA, investment, property, transaction, transfer, and deduction." Liam's smile widened. "I hope you've kept your receipts."

Blake swallowed hard. "I don't need to put up with this. I'm taking my business elsewhere."

"You do that." Liam slapped a hand on Blake's shoulder and gave it a squeeze. He leaned in to murmur quietly, but Joe heard every word. "If you, your father, or any of your associates come near Joe, his friends, or this shop, I'll know, and I will bury you so deep you'll wish you'd never laid eyes on him. Understood?"

Blake nodded fervently.

"Good. Now get the hell out."

Joe had no idea Blake could move that fast. The man all but fell over his own feet to flee from the place.

"I don't think he'll be bothering you anymore."

"Wow, that was… impressive," Joe admitted.

Liam chuckled. "I have my moments." He checked his watch and grimaced. "I have to go, but please, wait for me?"

Joe's heart swelled and he couldn't help his dopey grin. "Okay."

Liam reached into his pocket and pulled out a business card and pen. He turned the card over and jotted something down. "Here, my personal cell phone number." He handed the card to Joe, who took it, smiled at Liam's terrible handwriting, and placed it in his back pocket. The shop was full, and Joe could tell some of his nosy customers were watching, but his heart fluttered when Liam kissed his lips. It was brief, but wonderfully sweet.

With a wink and a wave to Bea and the kids behind the counter, Liam was off. Joe stood there for a moment watching as Liam climbed into a black Suburban. When it pulled away from the curb, Joe went back into the kitchen. He knew he'd get accosted and asked a billion questions, and he really didn't need to discuss his maybe love life out in the shop.

"So?" Bea asked. "Is he staying?"

"Staying?" Joe shrugged. "I don't think that's going to happen, Bea. I don't even know where he lives. Virginia, I think. He promised he'd be back as soon as he can to talk about us. Even if he wants to continue a relationship, how is that supposed to work with him in Virginia and me here?"

Bea walked over to him and cupped his face. "Sweetheart, it'll work out, you'll see. He's a good man, Joe. You can't let him slip through your fingers. Fight for him, for what you have. That man is crazy about you."

"He's a federal agent, Bea."

"And?"

"And he's… amazing."

Bea planted her hands on her hips, her expression no-nonsense. "So are you, Joe Applin. You are not going to run away from this." She sighed and put her hand to his cheek. "Honey, I have never seen you as happy as you've been while he was here. Take a chance, Joe. If there was ever a time to risk something, now is the time. He cares about you. You can make this work. The two of you, you need each other." She gave his cheek a kiss and left him to his own thoughts. He looked around the kitchen at the spotless stainless-steel table, workstation, and appliances. The spice rack caught his eye, and he walked over, smiling at how everything was in alphabetical order with neat little labels. Underneath it was the large sugar container, and Joe's heart swelled. How had he not noticed it before?

The container was labeled, like everything else, but instead of saying sugar, it said "Joe," and next to his name a little heart had been drawn in permanent marker. Joe chuckled. That goofball. Bea was right. He had to take a chance. Liam had asked Joe to wait for him, and that's what he would do. If it meant a chance with him, then Joe would do what he could. Joe needed Liam, and he was pretty certain Liam needed him too. They could make this work. He had to have faith in Liam, and although he wasn't accustomed to it, he had to have faith in himself.

Chapter Ten

THIS was all so surreal.

Joe sat in his garden, the sounds of the city almost muffled. He wasn't paying attention, too lost in thought. Bea had shooed him away from his own shop, demanding he take a break. She'd even threatened to lock him out if he didn't take some time off. From sunup to sundown, Joe was on his feet working away, keeping himself busy until he was too exhausted at the end of the night to do more than shower and go to bed.

Liam called every day at odd hours, apologizing for the not being able to come down. A little niggling part of Joe thought Liam was having second thoughts about them. They hadn't even discussed them. Liam felt guilty and Joe tried his best to assure him that he understood. The FBI was making arrests daily, rounding up members of the cartel, thanks to the intel Liam had gotten. Sometimes Liam would call in the middle of the night while he was sitting in a surveillance van. Joe didn't mind the lateness. He was grateful to hear Liam's voice.

Was this what it would be like if they were together? Liam off somewhere, unable to give him details of where he'd be or what he'd be doing, calling day and night? It wasn't like the FBI kept normal office hours. Having Liam away was hard, but getting to hear his voice raised Joe's spirits like nothing else. Somehow it made the distance bearable. It was funny, how at first Joe feared Liam being away would show the cracks in a relationship that perhaps hadn't been there to begin with, but the longer Liam was away, the more Joe thought about him.

Bea, Donnie, and Elsie were also great at keeping his spirits up, getting him excited about revamping the shop. It was time for a new look. Nothing crazy, but something a little more modern with a small bakery like he'd always wanted. It was time to stop dreaming about what he wanted in his life and do something about it. They'd all put their heads together and browsed several design concepts and found a color combination Joe loved: rich red walls and decor, deep brown furniture, and apple-green accents. Considering the name of the shop and his surname, it would be silly not to go with an apple theme. Work would start next week, and Joe was looking forward to it.

"Hey, Joe!"

Joe smiled and stood. "Hey, Jules." He pulled her into an embrace and hugged her tight. "It's so good to see you."

"I'm so sorry I haven't been by. I've been rushed off my feet. Things have been kind of crazy."

Oh, you have no idea.

Joe sat with Jules, her red curls bouncing along with her in excitement. "I got a new job!" she said.

"That's fantastic, Jules!" Joe pulled her in for another hug. He was excited for her. Jules was such a hard worker, and she cared so much for those she helped. He was glad to see her lit up with joy. Any hospital or clinic would be lucky to have her. "I'm so happy for you. You deserve it."

"Thank you. It's down at NYC Presbyterian Hospital. I haven't stopped since." She looked around. "How's Tom? I kept meaning to call, but every time I picked up the phone someone needed something. They've been short on staff these last few weeks. So where's Tom?"

"He's, um, not here," Joe said, unable to help the disappointment in his voice.

Jules's smile fell away. "What happened, Joe?"

"How long do you have?" Joe muttered. She leaned over and patted his hand.

"As long as it takes. Tell me. What happened?"

Joe took a deep breath and proceeded to tell Jules everything that had happened since she was last in, from the break-in to the fake Feds, the fights, the shoot-outs, the kidnapping, all the way up until Tom's departure. "Oh, and his name's Liam. Liam Baker."

Jules stared at him. She was so still Joe was afraid he might have broken her.

"Jules?"

"Wow. I don't even know how to respond to that. My God, Joe. I'm away for a few weeks and you get mixed up in some kind of federal sting operation? Are you making up for lost time? That's crazy!"

"I know. Believe me, I know."

Her expression softened. "You fell in love with him."

Joe opened his mouth to deny it, but he couldn't bring himself to. "Am I being an idiot?"

Jules shook her head. "Joe, you're one of the most sensible people I know. Tom—I mean, Liam—is a good man. I don't think he's the type to mince words or string someone along. I remember the way he looked at you. The man's got it bad for you. If he asked you to wait for him, then he'll be back. Listen to your heart. It's gotten you this far."

"Yeah, well, it hasn't got the greatest track record of reliability," Joe huffed.

"Joe." Jules met his gaze, her expression somber. "Don't make me send Bea after you, because you know I will."

Joe narrowed his eyes at her. "You wouldn't." She arched an eyebrow. Dang it, she would. He stood a better chance against a trained assassin than he did Bea. She was still telling him she told him so. "All right. Fine."

"Good." She smiled smugly and stood, giving his cheek a kiss. "I have to go, but I'll call you."

"Hi."

Joe stood and turned, his heart pounding at the sight of Liam standing there, dressed casually in dark jeans, a black T-shirt, and black leather jacket, like the first day they'd met.

"Hi." Joe felt silly. Just because Tom's name wasn't Tom didn't mean he was different, or that Joe didn't feel the same way about him. Yet everything *was* different.

Jules gave Joe a wink before heading to the side door and giving Liam a hug. "It's good to see you. I'm glad you got your memory back."

Liam hugged her back. "It's good to see you, Jules."

"Well, I'll leave you two to talk. Joe, call me if you need anything." She waved good-bye and was gone before Joe could say another word. He really should say something.

"I guess this must all seem a little boring now."

Liam smiled warmly and walked to Joe, giving him a sweet kiss. Joe melted against him. How he'd missed that warmth. Liam pulled Joe down with him as he sat on the stone bench. "Joe, I can assure you nothing about you is boring."

"I guess you'll be heading back home. To Virginia, if that's where your home is."

Liam nodded. "We're still wrapping things up, and I have a mountain of paperwork. Funny thing is, Virginia's where home was. Now I'm not so sure."

Was it too much to hope for? "Oh?" Joe held his breath as Liam turned to face him. He took Joe's hand in his, his silver eyes filled with affection.

"Before we get to that, there's something I need to tell you."

"Oh God, you're married. I knew it. Of course you are. Look at you." Joe shook his head, his heart sinking. It was stupid to think a guy like Liam was—

"I'm not married. Unless you count my job. We've been in a pretty intense relationship for years, and I think it's time we saw other people." Liam gave him a cheeky smile. "Break the news I kind of met someone."

Joe chuckled. A huge weight lifted off his shoulders, and he couldn't help his dopey grin. "You said you needed to tell me something. Why couldn't you tell me over the phone?"

Liam's smile fell away, and Joe braced himself.

"I needed to tell you this in person, so I hope you forgive me for waiting this long." Liam took a deep breath and let it out slowly before speaking up again. Whatever it was, it was important. "A few years ago, I came across a beautiful man who was in a good deal of trouble. When I reached him, he looked right at me. He had eyes like the ocean. Before I could say a word, he passed out. Every night at the hospital, I'd stay by his bedside and play old jazz tunes. I'd talk to him, keep him company. And then one day I received the call I'd been waiting for, and I was off to DC. I hated leaving him, knew I was giving up something good, but I was young and I wanted to help people like him. A few days later, the hospital called to inform me my dream guy was awake and would be fine."

Joe couldn't believe what he was hearing. When he spoke, his voice was almost a whisper. "Baker… It was *you*. You're Officer Baker."

Liam smiled bashfully. "I thought about you every day after that. Wondering what it might have been like if I'd stayed in New York. If I'd been there when you woke up. When this job came up in the city, I jumped at the chance. Not because of what it would do for my career, but because I might see you again. I knew I couldn't make contact, but sometimes I'd sit across the street with a cup of coffee and watch you go about your day."

Joe gasped. "You drank someone else's coffee?" He narrowed his eyes. "I don't think I like you anymore."

Liam chuckled. "Sorry."

"So what happened that night when you ended up in the garden?"

"I was in the neighborhood when I got the call to make the drop. That's when I realized I was being followed. I managed to give him the slip and then surprised him. That's why my knuckles were bruised. Knocked the guy out. Chances were the guy wasn't alone. I needed to stash the SD card, somewhere it would be safe. You came to mind. I jumped the gate and hid it in the pot of pink geraniums. I was about to leave when they whacked me on the back of the head. I'm guessing something or someone interrupted them, because they left me there."

"Can I ask you something?"

"Of course."

"Why didn't you come see me? Or call me? I tried looking for you everywhere. When I finally found your precinct, they said you were no longer on the force. I couldn't find anything else on you after that."

Liam looked remorseful. "You were moving on with your life. I didn't want to bring that pain back to you. Plus, I was scared."

Scared? Joe found it hard to believe Liam could be scared of anything. "Of what?"

"That once I talked to you I wouldn't be able to let you go." Liam met Joe's gaze and brought his hand to his lips for a kiss. "I had a lot going on at the time, and I was getting ready to go undercover. Had to have my head in the game or a lot of people could get hurt. The thought of you getting hurt because of me? I couldn't have that."

Joe thought about everything Liam had said about his job and his home in Virginia. It was a risk, putting his heart out there, but looking at Liam now, at those familiar silver eyes, Joe knew he would regret it if he didn't try.

"I was wondering if maybe you'd be interested in making some new memories. Ones that include me." Joe chanced a glimpse at Liam, his smile stealing Joe's breath away. Liam leaned in to kiss Joe's lips, sweet, slow, and filled with a need Joe had never felt from anyone.

"I'm pretty sure I lost my heart to you a long time ago, Joe, and even if all I had were memories of you, it would be more than enough for me." Liam put his hand to Joe's cheek. "How about tomorrow I come down on my lunch hour."

Joe frowned. "You're going to fly in by helicopter for lunch?" There was a wicked gleam in Liam's silver eyes. What wasn't he telling Joe?

"I was thinking about driving. And if you ever fancy meeting me for lunch, you can drop by the Federal Plaza down on Lafayette.

Lafayette? "Wait, but I thought you worked out of Virginia."

"I did. I put in for a transfer to the New York office. Figured it was time to come home." Liam placed his hand to Joe's cheek. "Now that I found my way home. That's what took me so long. I was waiting for the transfer to come through. I wanted to surprise you."

"You're moving to New York?" Joe's heart was all but ready to burst out of his chest.

"Yep. Maybe you can help me find a new apartment. Somewhere close to a place I can get some good coffee and the best pie in town served up by a gorgeous guy with eyes like the ocean."

Joe could barely contain his smile. "How about a slightly awkward guy who only has eyes for a certain sexy Fed?"

"Deal." Liam wrapped his arms around Joe and brought him in for the sweetest most wonderful kiss

Joe had ever experienced. Just when he thought Liam couldn't surprise him anymore, he'd found a way to sweep Joe off his feet. To think all those years ago, Liam entered his life. The very first time Liam saved him. Was that why being with him seemed familiar? And now Liam transferred to New York to be with him. Joe pulled back to meet Liam's gaze. He had to be sure.

"Is this what you want?"

Liam ran his thumb over Joe's bottom lip. "I let you go once. I won't make that mistake again. Will you forgive me for not telling you sooner about who I was?"

Joe wrapped his arms around Liam, his smile just for the amazing man in his arms. "If you promise not to get whacked on the head and forget me."

Liam threw his head back and laughed. When he looked at Joe, his eyes were filled with adoration. "I think I can do that."

"Liam?" Joe swallowed hard. He forced himself to hold Liam's gaze.

"Yeah?"

"I love you."

Liam's dazzling smile washed away any fears or insecurities Joe might have had left. "I love you too, Joe."

They kissed, and Joe gave himself over to the warmth and excitement spreading through him. He'd spent so much time running from his past, unaware of how it would not only catch up with him, but end up in his arms.

Coming in May 2016

DREAMSPUN DESIRES

#9

Duke in Hiding by M.J. O'Shea

Every gentleman has something to hide.

Meeting Heath Blackwood, a gorgeous English farmer, is probably the most exciting thing to ever happen to small-town landscaper Theo Brody, who has lived in quiet Mapleton, New Hampshire, all his life. The sexy and secretive Brit shakes the foundations of his orderly world as they are swept up in a springtime romance neither can resist.

But Heath's secrets run deeper than Theo ever imagined. He's actually Heathcliffe Pierrepont Blackwood, Seventh Duke of Kingston, in hiding from recent death threats. Suddenly there's more separating them than the Atlantic Ocean, and Theo doubts he'll ever fit in with English nobility. Though Heath and Theo are opposites in almost every way, their love might bridge the gap—if they're willing to take the risk.

#10

The Cattle Baron's Bogus Boyfriend by Nicki Bennett

It might be a sham to his boss, but it's all too real to him.

Administrative assistant Jonah Hollis has nurtured a hopeless crush on his boss, millionaire cattle rancher Lincoln Courtwright, ever since he started working for him. But hope is kindled when Linc and beautiful rodeo star Melissa Cutler break up just weeks before the biggest event of the Dallas social season, the Cattle Baron's Ball, and Linc asks Jonah to accompany him in her place.

Is it all a ploy to make Melissa jealous? Can Jonah fit into Linc's world? It takes some encouragement from his roommates and his best friend, Caylee, for Jonah to agree. Before long, Jonah dares to believe Linc might just feel something for him… until interfering family and a series of misunderstandings threaten his fragile dream of happiness.

www.dreamspinnerpress.com

Now Available

DREAMSPUN DESIRES

#3

The Stolen Suitor by Eli Easton

All of Clyde's Corner, Montana, knows local dandy Chris Ramsey will marry Trix Stubben, young widow and heir to the richest ranch in the area. But one woman isn't too keen on the idea. Mabe Crassen wants to get her hands on that ranch, so she sets her older son to court Trix, and her younger son, Jeremy, to distract Chris and lure him astray.

Jeremy Crassen thinks his mother's scheme is crazy. But he wants desperately to go off to college, which Mabe will agree to—if he seduces Chris. How will shy, virginal, secretly gay Jeremy attract Chris, who seems determined to do the right thing and marry Trix? Jeremy can't compete with a rich *female* widow. Or can he?

#4

The Lone Rancher by Andrew Grey

Aubrey Klein is in real trouble—he needs some fast money to save the family ranch. His solution? A weekend job as a stripper at a club in Dallas. For two shows each Saturday, he is the star as The Lone Rancher.

It leads to at least one unexpected revelation: after a show, Garrett Lamston, an old friend from school, approaches the still-masked Aubrey to see about some extra fun… and Aubrey had no idea Garrett was gay. As the two men dodge their mothers' attempts to set them up with girls, their friendship deepens, and one thing leads to another.

Aubrey know his life stretching between the ranch and the club is a house of cards. He just hopes he can keep it standing long enough to save the ranch and launch the life—and the love—he really hopes he can have.

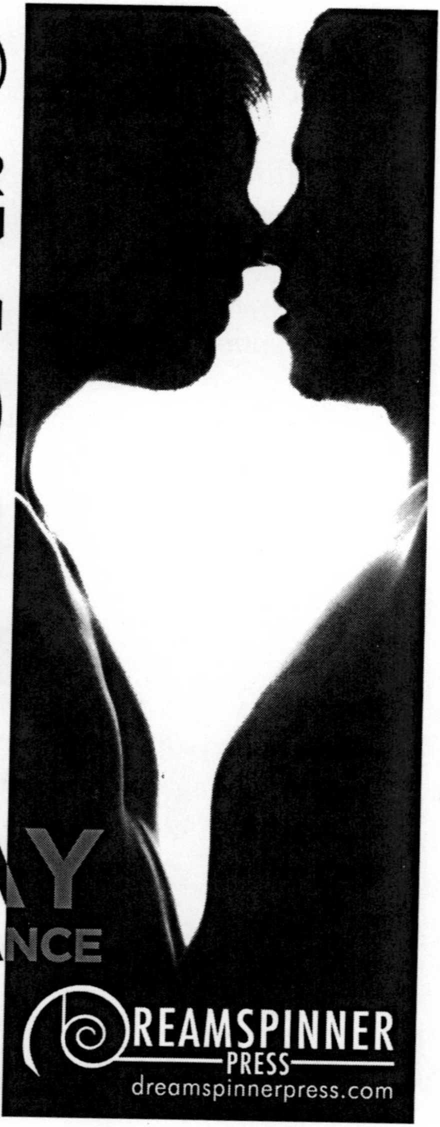

Lightning Source UK Ltd.
Milton Keynes UK
UKOW03f1133100517
300894UK00001B/1/P